Black Damp Century

by

Kerry George

ART or NAN.

Thank you

Kerry George

5-11-13

Published by Four Cats Publishing

Cover illustration and design by Tonya Foreman

ISBN-10: 0615677584
ISBN-13: 978-0-615-67758-3

For Shirley,
The toughest miner I ever met

TABLE OF CONTENTS

Acknowledgments   ix

Prologue   xi

Chapter 1: Fatal Encounter   3

Chapter 2: Clara's Adventure   9

Chapter 3: Miners and Liars   13

Chapter 4: A Brawl to the Death   19

Chapter 5: Karl's Education   23

Chapter 6: The Joining   27

Chapter 7: Bella's Agony   31

Chapter 8: Buck's World   35

Chapter 9: Depressing Depression   41

Chapter 10: Hopes and Fears   47

Chapter 11: Storm Clouds   53

Chapter 12: War's Unending Destruction   57

Chapter 13: Lost Love, Lost Life   63

Chapter 14: Jesse's World   67

Chapter 15: Grandpa's Ultimatum   71

Chapter 16: What Can I Do?   73

Chapter 17: The Master   75

Chapter 18: Choiceless Life   79

Chapter 19: The Shift   83

Chapter 20: In an Instant   103

Chapter 21: Clarity and Shame   107

Chapter 22: Disaster and Rebirth   111

Chapter 23: The Adjustment   117

Chapter 24: This Is My Union   119

Chapter 25: Another Way   123

Chapter 26: Black Gold   127

Chapter 27: The Great Coal Strike   129

Chapter 28: Legends Grow   133

Chapter 29: A Coal Miner's Wife   137

Chapter 30: Tragedy Strikes   139

Chapter 31: A New Position   143

Chapter 32: Change of Command   145

Chapter 33: Oakland Fantasy   153

Chapter 34: Georges Creek   157

Chapter 35: Working Women   165

Chapter 36: Preachers and Prophets   167

Chapter 37: War Clouds   173

Chapter 38: Autumn Glory   179

Chapter 39: The Breather   185

Chapter 40: The West Virginia Feast   195

Chapter 41: Dance of the Bureaucrats   199

Chapter 42: The Conspirators   201

Chapter 43: Friends and Enemies   203

Chapter 44: I Don't Understand   209

Chapter 45: Music and Gunfire   213

Chapter 46: Some You Win, Some You Lose   217

Chapter 47: The Malady of Frustration   219

Chapter 48: Plotting Friends   223

Chapter 49: The Never Ending Inspection   225

Chapter 50: You Don't Control Me   231

Chapter 51: The Closeout   235

Chapter 52: Mindless Men   237

Chapter 53: The Last Straw   245

Chapter 54: Friends and Enemies   251

Chapter 55: The Calm Before the Storm   255

Chapter 56: To Live or Die   261

Chapter 57: Waiting and Worrying   265

Chapter 58: Destiny's Circle   271

Chapter 59: The Accounting   273

Chapter 60: Do I or Don't I?   277

Chapter 61: You Reap What You Sow   279

ACKNOWLEDGMENTS

I would like to thank the following: My father who drove me everywhere I needed to go for researching this book. A special thanks to my wife, Christine, and daughter, Carrie. They had to put up with many long hours of my self-imposed exile. My many friends and family who read the early draft of this book. Their advice and critique are deeply appreciated. Don Hart, for his vast knowledge and experience; his suggestions were invaluable. Linda Hart for her editing skills and technical advice; without her the book would never have seen the light of day. Tonya Foreman, artist extraordinaire, whose abilities are displayed on the cover of this book. I would also like to thank John McCutcheon, singer-songwriter, for the use of the lyrics to his song "Step By Step". Lastly, I would like to thank the Ruth Enlow Library, Oakland, MD; Puskarich Public Library of Cadiz, OH; Ohio County Public Library, Wheeling, WV; Public Library of Steubenville and Jefferson County, Steubenville, OH; and the Kanawha County Public Library of Charleston, WV. Their assistance in the research for this book is greatly appreciated.

PROLOGUE

In America's coalfields in the 1920s, mine workers were virtual slaves of the owners. They were paid in private money called script, redeemable only at the Company Store, also operated by these same mine owners. Miners paid inflated prices for food, clothing, and any other item sold at the store. They were even required to buy the black powder used to blast loose their employer's coal. Without hard currency, they were unable to move freely in the country.

Mining conditions were deplorable; explosions and fires were commonplace. Miners died by the thousands. Hundreds of thousands more worked in intolerable conditions. As in most situations of this kind, a revolt was in the offing.

The politics of the time favored the coal operators. From President Warren Harding to Governor Ephraim F. Morgan of West Virginia, politicians believed business owners were beyond reproach and the employees were mere rabble-rousers. Many of the mine owners hired enforcers to control their employees, discourage unions and glean information. Detective agencies were especially useful in providing owners with these kinds of "services."

The Baldwin-Felts Detective Agency based in Bluefield, West Virginia, provided guards and police for many of the nation's coalfields. They did the bidding of the coal mine owners. Their primary mission was to prevent unionization in the mines, and they were ruthless in carrying out that mission.

On May 19, 1920, an incident occurred in Matewan, West Virginia, that would have far reaching consequences. The Stone Mountain Coal Company was in the midst of a strike to unionize. Twelve Baldwin-Felts detectives arrived to carry out evictions of miners within the community. The Felts group was led by Albert and Lee Felts, brothers of the agency's owner. The men were confronted by the town's police chief Sid Hatfield and its mayor Cabell Testerman. The brothers were unaware they had been surrounded by armed coal miners. Gunshots rang out and when the smoke cleared Albert and Lee Felts lay dead, along with Cabell Testerman. Seven detectives and three townspeople died that day.

Police Chief Sid Hatfield and his deputies were brought to trial for murder and were found not guilty. During the next year Hatfield gained legendary status among the miners. But the owner of the Baldwin-Felts Detective Agency was determined to avenge his brothers. Felts colluded with the mine owners to have a summons issued for Hatfield and his chief deputy Ed Chamber. They were to appear at the McDowell County Courthouse in Welch, West Virginia. The men came accompanied by their wives and were unarmed. As they climbed the steps of the courthouse, they were met by a large group of Baldwin-Felts men. The detectives gunned down both men in front of their wives.

An enraged group of miners began to pour into the capital of West Virginia at Charleston, demanding action by the new governor, Ephraim Morgan. The Governor had only a few state police to maintain order, and the situation soon grew out of hand. Lacking a state National Guard, the Governor appealed to President Warren Harding for assistance, which was not forthcoming.

Later, the miners assembled on Lens Creek, at Marmet, West Virginia. From there they began the march on Mingo and Logan Counties. Their intention was to force unionization on the southern West Virginia coalfields.

A great obstacle stood in the miners' way. The sheriff of Logan County, Don Chafin, had sworn that no armed miner would set foot in his county. Chafin then controlled the largest private army in the United States; he had two thousand men under arms. They were well trained and well provisioned by the Logan County Coal Operators Association. This force was augmented by hundreds more paid strikebreakers and townspeople. Chafin began putting up breastworks on Blair Mountain, a defensive line that would stretch for over a mile.

The miners' numbers were estimated from three thousand to well over fifteen thousand. The two sides clashed on August 25, 1921, and the battle raged until September 2, 1921 when martial law was declared by President Harding.

The total dead and wounded has never been confirmed. It is estimated that over one hundred and fifty were killed and many hundreds wounded. The miners carried many of their comrades off the field, and as far as their casualties, the miners would never tell.

After the battle, nine hundred eighty-five miners were charged with murder or conspiracy to commit murder. Many were acquitted, but a large number were found guilty and languished in prison until they were paroled in 1925.

The aftermath of the battle was devastating to the United Mine Workers of America and the American labor movement. They would not begin to recover until the late 1930s.

The Twentieth Century was a time of great turbulence for the coal miners, mine owners, and the government agents involved. Great changes were coming. This is their story as seen through the eyes of two fictional families.

PART I:
REVOLUTION

The organized workers of America, free in their industrial life, conscious partners in production, secure in their home and enjoying a decent standard of living, will prove the finest bulwark against the intrusion of alien doctrines of government.

—John L. Lewis, President of the United Mine Workers of America, 1920-1960

Black damp — a mining term that basically means oxygen starved atmosphere.

CHAPTER 1
FATAL ENCOUNTER

You load sixteen tons, what do you get?
Another day older and deeper in debt,
Saint Peter, don't you call me, 'cause I can't go;
I owe my soul to the company store...

   —Tennessee Ernie Ford, 1955

The downright fanatic is nearer to the heart of things than
the cool and slippery disputant.

   —Edwin Hubbell Chapin

HATFIELD, PICTURESQUE MOUNTAINEER,
SLAIN IN GUN FIGHT

   —*Wheeling Register*, August 2, 1921

  William Storm was resting his back against a tree with a rifle across his lap. He was hot, dirty, and angry. But the worst thing for him was the waiting. How did he get here? A fly buzzed near his ear. It was one of thousands of little creatures that were making his life miserable. He caught a glimpse of movement in the shadowed meadow. Two deer had stepped into the open to graze. For a few brief moments he was distracted from his torment.

  Storm's mind flew from one thought to another. First was the disgust he felt with his traveling companions.

3

His anger over being forced into this intolerable situation was the second. Then he thought of Bella, his lovely and very pregnant wife, just days away from giving birth. He fingered the white scarf that he wore and smiled. He glanced at the deer. They were not aware of him. The harmony of the scene relaxed him. If only men could live in such a state.

But after a few moments Storm found it hard to stay still. He was in a quandary. He had brought Bella to visit his father, and then it began. An assassination had turned his world upside down. A man named Sid Hatfield had been gunned down, igniting a firestorm in the hills of West Virginia.

Hatfield was a darling of the coal miners. He was almost a godlike symbol to the men. His murder was like pouring gasoline on a smoldering fire. Men were coming with guns to kill or be killed.

Storm's father was the President of the Logan County Coal Operators Association and had demanded that William lead a scouting party into the hills to see what the miners were up to and to gauge the size of their force. He had protested strongly, but to no avail.

Three men were picked to accompany him. All worked for the Baldwin-Felts Detective Agency. One of those men was named Smallie. He made no secret of his hatred for the coal miners. His older brother had been killed at what had become known as the Matewan Massacre. He was a deeply scarred man. The other two were what Storm would have described as bullies with badges. As long as they had power and guns, they had courage.

Things had not gone well since Storm was sent on

the scouting mission. Smallie had continually argued with him. It became evident to both men that a confrontation was in the making.

Storm thought about Bella. When he was released from the Army at the end of the Great War, he had returned to college to complete his law degree. There he met Bella McGinnis. She was from a small town in Maryland. Her father was also a coal mine owner. They had decided to settle in Maryland after their marriage. For him it was an escape from the constant violence of southern West Virginia. Western Maryland did not have the labor strife that plagued Logan.

Their visit was supposed to be a short interlude before the birth of their first child, and now it had been extended for nearly a month. He had been trying to leave when his father forced him into this misery.

Storm was unaware that another man lay not forty yards from him. He too was hot, dirty, and angry. He was silently watching every move that Storm made.

His thoughts were interrupted by the crack of a branch. The deer jumped and ran out of sight. His eyes moved to the trail across the clearing. He saw two of the men he had been waiting for coming towards him. They were dragging something.

"What the hell you got there?" Storm yelled.

"A prisoner." The big man answered.

As they got closer he could see that they were pulling a young girl along behind them.

She was strikingly pretty, with long dark hair. But what struck him the most was the terrified look on her face.

"Are you two crazy?" Storm's voice was rising.

"We stumbled onto her about a mile back. Thought it would be a good idea to have some insurance. You know, just in case."

"Take that rope off her neck."

They hesitated. He raised his rifle menacingly. They finally complied.

"Come here, girl." Storm directed.

Like a little puppy she complied. She was some sight. Her dress was ripped, barely covering her and she was racked with sobs. He guessed her age at around fifteen or sixteen.

"Where do you come from, girl?"

"We live near Sharples," she answered, quivering.

"What the hell are you doing out in these woods knowing the trouble that's coming?"

"Ma didn't think there was no danger yet. She wanted me to get news of what was happening."

The man lying in the shadows had tensed when he saw the men dragging the girl into the clearing. He was ready to kill Storm and his men but quickly calmed himself when he saw one of the men protecting the girl.

Storm sensed that the big fellow was starting to raise his rifle.

"I'd be putting that gun down if I were you." Storm said as he pointed his gun at the man's chest.

"Take it easy there, Storm. You look a little shaky with that there gun." The big man replied.

"Tell you what, I bet I can't miss you from here," Storm smiled.

The little man finally spoke up.

"Storm, you some kind of fool or what? You's supposed to be on our side, ain't ya?"

Storm studied the two men. They were not as

menacing as Smallie but they were still dangerous. If the Great War had taught him anything, it was that mainly two kinds of men came home: the remorseful and the indifferent; these men were the indifferent with no regard for any life.

The girl watched this drama play out. She was deeply afraid. At the same time she was intrigued by Storm's defense of her. She wondered many things. Why was he defending her? No man like him had ever even spoken to her before. And why was he wearing that stupid white scarf around his neck when it was so hot?

"You wait till Smallie gets here." The big man yelled.

"To hell with Smallie. We are letting her go now." Storm said as he gestured towards the girl.

Then something struck him hard in the back, propelling him ten feet. He landed in a sitting position. He stared down at his chest where blood was pouring from an open wound soiling his white scarf. He glanced up to see Smallie stepping into the clearing, smoke coming from the barrel of his rifle. He fell back to the ground dead.

"Smallie, are you nuts? How we ever gonna explain this?" The big man whined.

Smallie just glared at the two men as he moved towards the girl. He had gone crazy since the death of his brother. His sole purpose was to inflict pain on coal miners. It was he who had laid the barrel of his pistol against Hatfield's head while he was dying on the courthouse steps. The men around him would always remember that crazy smile on his face as he pulled the trigger blowing Hatfield's brains out. He had then turned to Hatfield's wife, tipped his hat, said "Mum" and walked away.

"Boys, do you think I would let that son-of-a-bitch

deprive us of a little entertainment? Repeat after me: Storm got killed by miners. You got it. Anyways, I was tired of that bastard."

Smallie walked up to the girl and with one quick jerk tore the dress from her body. She did not whimper or run. She attacked him trying to claw his eyes out. He struck her so hard that she fell unconscious.

Then the coal miner in hiding fired three quick shots. Smallie and his two cohorts died without a sound.

CHAPTER 2
CLARA'S ADVENTURE

What a day may bring a day may take away.

—Thomas Fuller

MINERS GATHER TO INVADE MINGO

—*Wheeling Register*, August 21, 1921

Karl Kamin stepped from the wood line and walked over to where the men lay. He checked all four bodies. He assured himself that they were all dead. He then turned his attention to the girl. She was still out cold. He picked her up and carried her from the clearing. A little stream ran nearby. He removed his own shirt and covered her nakedness. He soaked his bandanna and wiped her face.

She came to with a start. She was fighting like a bobcat.

"Easy, easy. You are safe. No one can harm you now." Kamin's words calmed her quickly.

But she eyed him warily and looked all around.

"Where are the others? How did I get here? Who are you?"

"I am a friend. The others are gone. My name is Karl Kamin."

She seemed to settle down. He made no moves towards her, but she was still leery of him.

He gave her a drink of water from a flask he

carried. She could not believe how thirsty she was. She began to relax. Then the tears came. Through sobs she began to explain what happened.

"My mom wanted me to go into Madison and see if we could get some news about what was happening. I was on a trail about a mile from our house when those men grabbed me. I was real scared, Mister. I thought those men would kill me. Around here they treat us lower than dogs."

"Where are your men folk?" Kamin asked.

"All dead. My Pa and brothers were all killed at Monongah."

The name sent shudders down Kamin's spine. Every coal miner was aware of that mine. The worst mining disaster in the nation's history happened there in December of 1907. Three hundred and sixty-two men and boys died that day. That was the official version anyway. At that time they did not have any check in and check out system in place. No one knew how many were in the mine when it exploded. Estimates ranged between the official number and five hundred. Fathers took sons into the mine with them and bosses hired men right off the street. Many of the immigrants were without families and no one reported them missing. Only God knew the true toll.

"What's your name, girl?"

"Clara Dibello. My mom and I live by ourselves. Some friend of my father's lets us use a cabin for nothing. Mom and I do odd jobs for spending money when we can get it. Mom does sewing and laundry for the mine bosses. I help out on a local farm for milk and cheese."

He remembered thinking how solidly she was built as he carried her here. It was nearly dark so he decided to remain where there were.

10

"We'll rest here till morning. Then I will take you home."

When Clara woke at dawn she saw Kamin resting against a tree. She had not realized how big he was. She thought he was at least 6 feet. There was not an ounce of fat on him. She stared at him for many minutes. He looked pretty to her. She could not guess his age. She figured he was younger than he looked. He was wearing bib overhauls, a big red bandanna, and boots. She was aware that he had given her his shirt. Now she could see his muscled arms and chest. Like all young girls she was inquisitive. She stepped closer and reached up, shaking him. She was not prepared for what happened next.

Kamin came awake with a start. He flung out his arms knocking the girl to the ground. She let out a squeal. Within a second or two he realized what had happened.

"Hey, Mister, are you nuts? I just wanted to talk." Clara was wide eyed and feeling new fear.

Kamin got up. "Girl, don't ever be waking a man with a gun in his hands like that. I could have killed you."

He walked over to the stream and drank.

"Let's be movin'." He started to walk without a look back.

She yelled at him. "Mister, take me to Madison. That's where I was headed when I got caught."

Madison it would be. That was where he had been told to return to. Clara guessed it to be about 12 miles from where they stood.

CHAPTER 3
MINERS AND LIARS

Facts are stubborn things.

—Tobias Smollett

SEVEN HUNDRED MEN JOIN MINERS, MOTHER JONES WILL ADDRESS ARMED FORCES

—*Wheeling Register*, August 23, 1921

They trudged through the woods for several hours with Clara as his guide back to Madison. He liked the mountains but was still awed by the steep ridges towering over the valleys.

When he started out from Marmet, he was spellbound by the narrowness of the valley floors. A creek, the railroad tracks, a dirt road running alongside, and the few company houses lining the tracks lay before them. Everything had the drab look of most mining towns. Coal dust layered everything. It coated the houses and the leaves of the trees, and it clung to the people.

The miners had commandeered trains to transport the men up Lens Creek. They trickled in by tens and then hundreds. They all sensed that something of great significance was about to happen. For Kamin it represented adventure. He was indeed sympathetic with the miners' plight since he had been a miner from the age of eight. Being here was another way of expressing his independence. He would not allow anyone to control him.

He had settled in a little valley in Ohio. He worked at a mine called Robeyville, just outside of Adena. When word came of Hatfield's death, he packed up his pistol and rifle. He started out for Charleston, West Virginia. He had not even bothered to let the people at the mine know.

When he arrived at Charleston he found that the men had moved on to Marmet. What he found there was a mob. No leaders, no organization, and no clue about how to proceed. He heard the names Keeney and Blizzard, the bosses in the Union. But he never met them. Just like the other miners he met, he kept guessing, "What next?"

As the men meandered through those formidable hills on their way to Logan, each had a single thought on his mind. Avenge Sid Hatfield. It was going to be a hot time in Logan when they arrived.

Kamin thought about how he had stumbled across those men and the girl. No one had told him to go scouting. He just up and did it. It seemed the right thing for an army to be doing. He kept forgetting this was no army. It was just a bunch of angry men with guns.

His mind drifted back to those men he had killed. He had no qualms about what he did. He had been in enough fights in the trenches of the Great War to know that you never gave an enemy an even break. He never fought to be fair. He fought to win and survive. He and the girl were alive and safe that was all that mattered.

"There it is!" Clara yelled.

Her voice jarred him back to the present. She was

smiling at him and pointing to the town. With her face awash in sunlight she was absolutely beautiful. They walked into Madison and were stunned by how many people were there. Men were lying about everywhere. It seemed there was a steady roar from thousands of voices. They were all talking at once and all incoherent. Another sight that greeted them was the amount of glass covering the streets and sidewalks. The men had ransacked every store taking whatever they needed for the coming fight.

They came upon one small group of men listening to a black man playing a dulcimer. He was singing an eerily haunting tune. His song was so mesmerizing that they both listened intently.

"Step by step," the man began. The words were so good Clara tried to memorize them.

They spoke of unity, strength and courage.

"Step by step, the longest march can be won, can be won. Many stones can form an arch, singly none, singly none." When the man stopped singing Kamin walked up to him.

Putting out his hand he said, "The name's Kamin."

"I'm Tom Katts, pleased to meet ya."

"We really liked your song." Kamin answered, pointing to the girl standing next to him.

"They are just a simple old coal miner's thoughts."

They congratulated each other on being a part of such a godly undertaking and parted company.

Kamin soon spotted a group of women standing on a wooden sidewalk in front of a small store. He led Clara to them. They were watching the miners milling around the town.

"Can you ladies take care of this young girl? She has had a mighty rough time."

15

"Clara!" One of the women yelled. She rushed past Kamin nearly forcing him from the wooden steps. Clara looked over her shoulder to see Kamin walking away without another glance.

Kamin started to wander through the streets to see if he could find anyone he knew. He did not. What he found was the same mass confusion that he had seen earlier.

A man asked him if he was hungry. Kamin took some meat and bread from the guy, thanked him, and kept wandering through the town. He stopped to listen to some men talking about Mother Jones. She was another folk hero of the miners.

Her real name was Mary Harris Jones. The mine owners and the politicians considered her the most dangerous woman in the country. For years she had been championing the rights of the coal miners. They called her Mother and she called them Her Boys. If her boys did not stand up for themselves, she would shame them into doing the right thing.

Kamin was shocked when he heard the men say that she had lied to them. It happened near Marmet. She had come to speak and told them that she had a change of mind about the march that she had instigated. She told them that she was holding a telegram from President Harding and he had promised to right all the wrongs done to them.

Keeney and Blizzard, the Union bigwigs, jumped up and challenged what Mother Jones had said. Keeney went into Charleston and contacted the President's office by telegraph. They verified that no telegram had been sent to Mother Jones. Caught in a lie, she had to leave in disgrace, never again to have the stature she once held.

16

Kamin thought he understood why she had lied. She had single handedly been the cause of this march. It was her words that fanned the flame of rebellion. The realization that she was sending men to their deaths probably shocked her back into reality. He could not be too condemning of a person who lied to save lives.

Another assembly came the following day. It was Saturday, August 27. The Union big shots held a quick meeting with a group of the men. The first skirmish had already occurred on August 25. They put out word that a vote was taken. The men were to return to their homes. They had hoped to defuse the situation. So the men began to think of leaving. The following day rumors started to spread through the camps that Sheriff Don Chafin's men were killing women and children in Sharples, West Virginia. Sheriff Chafin controlled Logan County and had sworn that no miner would set foot in Logan County carrying a gun.

That did it. The men regrouped and headed to Blair Mountain. They had been lied to for the last time. When Kamin heard, he hoped that Clara was safe. He hated to think that he was the cause of her being in danger.

CHAPTER 4
A BRAWL TO THE DEATH

Now is the Winter of our discontent.

—William Shakespeare, *Richard III*, Act 3. Sc. 1

BLOODY OUTBREAK REPORTED

—*Wheeling Register*, August 30, 1921

Kamin was herded into a coal car along with hundreds of other men for the journey to Blair Mountain. The hijacked trains were used to move men and supplies to where they would do the most good. The foliage was dense in August, and it did well in concealing the movement of thousands of men.

Kamin found himself in the midst of what seemed like two or three thousand men. They slowly followed wooded trails that would lead them to Don Chafin and his army. The miners were nothing more than a mob. There were no squads, platoons, or companies; they were just a large phalanx pointed in the right direction.

What Kamin did not know was that his group was part of a large force attacking the right flank of Chafin's line, at a place called the South Crest. Another force was attacking the left flank on North Crest. With a token force driving right up the center, they might have been a mob, but they had a purpose.

Kamin was suddenly exposed to a wall of lead. He

had seen withering gunfire before. This was no less intense. The shooting was continuous. Chafin's men had a vast amount of automatic weapons with interconnected fields of fire. Karl squinted through the smoke and could not believe how many were wounded. He had no idea the number of dead. He had seen some, but if the wounded were any indication the number would be high.

The miners kept pressing the attack. The mine guards fought well but the miners numbers were beginning to tell. The battle raged all day and night. On Monday, August 29, Kamin found himself separated from the main force. He was with about twenty men. The firing had slowed somewhat and he took the time to rest against a big tree and light his pipe. It occurred to him that if he died, there would be no one to mourn him. It had never bothered him before. For some reason he thought of that girl.

He heard a plane flying over but could not see it for the foliage. Suddenly there was a large burst in the trees. Kamin felt a great stab of pain and then he lost consciousness.

Chafin had hired planes and pilots to bomb the miners. They were literally throwing bombs at the men. Chafin's line was in danger of being overrun. Tuesday morning word came that President Harding had issued a proclamation commanding the rebels to withdraw and return to their homes. The men refused to lay down their weapons. They feared being shot down by Chafin and his men. Finally the President of the United States declared martial law.

After a week of furious fighting it was over. The men would not fire on American troops. They were not at war with the United States just with the coal operators. This had not been a battle. It was a brawl. This had not been political. It had been personal. This would be the last time that thousands of guns would speak in anger on American soil.

The aftermath was horrendous for the miners and the Union. The mine owners had won. It was the miners who would go to jail. It was they who would lose everything. It was their wives and children who would suffer. But like the Phoenix, they would again rise from the ashes.

CHAPTER 5
KARL'S EDUCATION

Tis education forms the common mind;
Just as the twig is bent the tree's inclined.

—Alexander Pope, *Moral Essays*

Karl jumped when he heard his stepfather yell. "Dammit, boy, I said it's time to go." Kamin was only eight years old and he was being dragged into a life that he could not imagine. Today was to be his first day in a coal mine.

His family had come from Vigolo Vattaro, Italy. Like many of the families in Mount Carmel, Pennsylvania, they had come to work the mines. Karl's father Antonio Kaminetti was a good and honorable man. He was well liked in the community. His mother, Eva, was a quiet, rather frail woman.

Karl was the first generation of their family born in the United States and his father had great plans for him. Antonio and Eva dreamed of a good life for their Karl. Like most dreams this one ended unexpectedly. A massive rock fall at the Draco Mine destroyed it. It took hours to dig Antonio's body out from under the tons of rock that ended his life. At the time of his father's death Karl was six years old.

Within two years his mother remarried. Soon after, his new stepfather, Giovanni Marchi, began treating Eva and the boy horribly. He announced that Karl would be accompanying him to the mine. This was over Eva's strong objections. Giovanni wanted to use the extra few cents for anisette.

Karl and his stepdad walked from their small house to the mine which stood on the edge of town. Coal was a dirty business. It was early spring and you could see soot and coal dust everywhere.

Both were dressed for work in whatever was available. Each had on a cloth cap with a little teapot attached. The pot was loaded with grease ignited to give the workers light. The boy's lunch pail dragged the ground as they walked. The eight year old was just not big enough to hold it up.

Karl saw a man carrying a bird cage. He asked his stepfather, "What's that for?"

The man answered. "It's for the black damp. If there ain't no air, the canary dies. We don't."

They stood in line with other men waiting to load into small coal cars to be lowered down the slope and into the mine. Karl was frightened but tried not to show it. Giovanni never spoke, nor even looked at him. Karl did not know it was common for men to take their sons to work.

When they were lowered to the bottom of the slope he entered a very strange world. The first thing Karl discovered was how dark it was. Next he saw mules pulling coal cars to be taken out of the mine. They just plopped along as if they knew where they were going.

He tagged along behind his stepfather and the others till they arrived at what Giovanni called the faces. This was where they would work. They walked into one such place till they came to the solid coal. The wooded tracks came right up near the coal. Karl just stood there waiting. He was standing in an underground forest. There were literally thousands of posts supporting the roof.

Giovanni finally said, "We're gonna load coal into them cars, boy, and don't be putting any rock in there. The boss man checks each car and if he finds any stone he docks us the pay for the whole car. We get paid by how many tons we load. Understand, boy?"

The boy watched as the older man prepared to shoot down the coal. The first thing that he did was drill holes into the coal. This was done by using augers attached to a breast plate which Giovanni leaned against as he turned the augers and applied pressure. He then loaded the hole with black powder. The next step was to use a squib, something like a Roman candle. This was placed in the hole's opening and lit to ignite the powder. He moved the boy to a safe spot before lighting the squib. But before he could finish he heard a terrible rumble and screams. Giovanni went to see what happened with the boy scurrying behind. What they found were two dead men.

The men had been preparing their place to mine when a rock fall occurred. Both were killed instantly. All the men on the section had come running including their boss. They were able to get both men out from under the rocks fairly quickly. Then they began milling around talking about going out with the dead men. That was when the boss spoke up.

"You can't do them boys any good by going home. We got coal to mine. I'll fire the first one that heads towards the bottom. We'll take them out at quitting time. Now lay them in the gob." There was some moaning at this, but the men started to return to their work.

Karl's eyes were about as wide as they could be. He

was as frightened as he ever had been. He kept staring at the blood-spattered bodies that were lying alongside the track. Finally his stepfather spoke up.

"Come boy, back to work. We ain't making no money standing here."

The older man started to explain a little more about what they were doing.

"The gob the boss was talking about was stone we take out of the coal we load. We throw it alongside the track or leave it in the side cuts we make."

"But why didn't we take them men outside to their folks?" Karl choked.

"'Cause that boss said he'd fire us if we left. Now move. No more questions."

Karl helped load the car with coal. Finally the older man said, "Let's eat."

Karl did not feel like eating. He just leaned back against the coal and closed his eyes thinking of nothing but those two dead men lying a few feet away.

Karl heard someone calling his name and came wide awake knowing that his stepfather would be hitting him for falling asleep. But it was not his stepfather. It was a young girl. She looked really familiar. He started to say something but drifted right back to sleep.

CHAPTER 6
THE JOINING

Conscience is a mother-in-law whose visit never ends.

—Henry Louis Mencken

"He's awake, Ma! He's awake!"
Karl had been carried six miles from where he had been injured. By chance, he had been brought back to Clara. She and her mother had taken in three wounded men that day. Karl had lain unconscious for over a week. Clara did not recognized him at first. He was covered with blood from a severe head wound. She was stunned when her mother finished cleaning him. Clara finally saw the man's face.
"Ma, this is the man that saved me."
From that moment on Clara never left his side. She gave him sips of water. She tried to feed him chicken broth. She spoke to him constantly. She had tried everything she could think of to help him. The girl began to wonder if he would ever awaken. She had just been ready to leave his side and get something to eat when his eyes flew open for that brief second.
Karl Kamin had been at the place for two weeks. Clara insisted on tending him herself. Her mother did not like the attention that her daughter was showing the older man. Clara explained how he had saved her life, but her mother was not too impressed. All she had told her mother was that she was being badgered by some bullies and Kamin had freed her from them.

27

Clara was at the age when she still sought comfort from her mother but that was about all. This was the first time that Kamin had shown any sign of coming out of the coma, and with God's help she aimed to see that he got a whole lot better.

He was getting stronger each day and was taking small walks around the cabin. He was full of questions about what happened to the miners and how he had gotten to their cabin. He could understand the boys quitting the fight especially when federal troops had been brought in. He found himself enjoying his talks with the girl. He had never been this open with anyone in his life. He looked forward to seeing her. He had to think about this some more.

Clara's mother was a nice enough person, but Kamin sensed that she was very cool to him. More and more she had found some excuse to pull Clara from him. He had been the perfect gentleman. But it did not appear to make a difference to the girl's mother.

He decided to confront her. One day Clara had gone out on an errand. Karl walked up to the older woman.

"Can we talk?" He asked.

She stared at him rather coldly. "Go ahead and talk."

"I don't know why you are so angry at me. I try to be pleasant to you but it doesn't work." He stammered.

"I'll tell you why I'm angry. 'Cause you are going to hurt my daughter."

"I would never do anything to hurt Clara." He answered, shocked.

The older woman just shook her head. "Can't you see that she is falling in love with you?"

"I'm in love with her, too. That girl is more woman than I have ever met before. I want to marry her."

The woman was stunned. She was not thinking along that line. She had been worried about him toying with her daughter's affections. The next instant she thought of herself. She would be alone. She might never see Clara again.

As if to answer her questions he spoke. "If she will have me, I want you to come with us. I have fifty acres back in Ohio and a solid little cabin. If you don't come, Clara would be miserable without you."

It was as if a different woman stood in front of him. All of a sudden she was all smiles.

"Don't say anything to Clara, please. Let me ask her in my own way." He begged.

That afternoon he and Clara were walking near the creek.

"Clara there is some things I want you to know about me."

She started to interrupt but he went on.

"My real name is Kaminetti. I left home when I was fourteen years old. My ma died and I hated my stepdad. We got into a big fight and I left him lying in the middle of our kitchen. He was never going to lay a hand on me again."

She smiled. "You don't have to tell me these things."

"No, I want you to know. I done many things that I ain't proud of. Sometimes I drink. Sometimes I fight. I smoke and most of the time I cuss. But I'm a hard worker and I got me some ground. One more thing you need to know. I'm twice your age. The reason that I am telling you this is that I want you to marry me."

She lit up and flew right into his arms. Then she hesitated and stared back at the cabin.

He continued. "I want you and your mother to come back to Ohio with me. I want to build a life with you. I promise never to be mean to you and to always provide for you. Clara, I love you."

They kissed for the first time. Laughing with happiness, she dragged him back to her mother.

CHAPTER 7
BELLA'S AGONY

People hate, as they love, unreasonably.

—William Makepeace Thackeray

MARTIAL LAW HELD IN ABEYANCE
FOLLOWING MINERS' SUBMISSION

—*Wheeling Register*, September 4, 1921

Bella stood waiting on the veranda of her father-in-law's home. Word had come this morning that President Harding had declared martial law. The guns had fallen silent almost immediately. Logan was again safe. Harding had saved the day. Tired men had retired to the town. It had been twelve days since her beloved William had left her to do who knows what.

She sensed the presence of William's father as a hand went up to her shoulder.

"Don't be worrying, honey. He'll be along shortly." William Sr. said.

"Papa, it has been so many days and not a word." Bella answered.

They both stood in silence, each lost in their own world. The father too was worried. Word should have come from his son by now. They continued watching the mass of men coming into town. William Sr. had spoken to Chafin, their sheriff, about his son. Chafin said he would send men out to look for the scouts. In the seven days since the shooting started, Chafin had not once given his scouts a thought.

Clara winced as the child in her swollen belly kicked. The old man smiled.

"Is that boy beating to get out and meet his grandpa?"

"I think he is as anxious to be born as I want him to be."

Her thoughts turned back to William Jr. She just did not understand this violence. Her dad ran mines. They did not have any trouble. What her dad said went. Those foreigners who spoke all those strange languages believed her dad knew what was best for them. She began to understand why her dad referred to them as human chattel. Not much good for anything but following.

She noticed a group of men coming towards them. They were carrying something. As they got closer she saw a white scarf with a dark stain hanging from what they carried. She shuttered. The men had brought her husband to her lying atop an outhouse door. She began to scream.

Within two hours William Storm III was born. It was not to fanfares or trumpets blaring, but grief. Bella had gone into labor minutes after learning of her husband's death. Her father-in-law was deeply troubled. He had demanded answers. The men told him his son and his three companions had all been shot in the back. Bella's condition forestalled any hopes of an immediate accounting. As he stood there looking down on his new grandson he was torn between anguish and joy.

Bella was also torn. Something had snapped in her. She stared at her son, such a beautiful boy. What she felt was hate. Hate for every coal miner who lived. She wanted to avenge her beloved. Some day she would have revenge for the destruction of her life. Perhaps it would come through this child.

CHAPTER 8
BUCK'S WORLD

A rich man is nothing but a poor man with money.

—W. C. Fields

"Boy, it's time you learned my five rules of business. One, you are the boss, act like one. Two, intimidation works. Be mean as hell 'cause most men will be cowed. Three, when challenged attack immediately. Four, nothing is ever black or white, yes or no. Manipulate every situation to your advantage. Five, if you run up against a man or organization that you can't intimidate withdraw and attack from another direction. Remember this is your business not theirs."

Duffy McGinnis finished with one last caveat, "Your family is your life, boy."

Billy Storm only nine had listened with the enthusiasm of his youth. He had only one thing to say to his grandpa. "I ain't mean."

McGinnis laughed and said, "Give yourself a few years and life will make you that way."

McGinnis owned a small underground coal mine just outside of Lonaconing, Maryland. He had twenty men working, one shift a day, mining a coal seam called the Big Vein. He had over two hundred acres of this coal tied up and it was one of the few blocks not mined by the big companies at the turn of the century. The men who worked there were the desperate and the unskilled. No one else would hire them and McGinnis could not get anyone of quality because of his nature.

His mine was unsafe sending many a man to his death. Little Billy loved his grandfather but was extremely fearful of him. The old man was in his sixties with a wiry build. He always went unshaven and had to walk with a cane due to one of the many accidents that happened at his mine. He would go into his mine everyday just to see that his orders were carried out. He had one man he paid a few cents extra to watch over the other men's work.

They stayed at the mine for about four hours that day. It was Billy's first time to go inside the mine with his granddad. He would never forget the smell; it reminded him of an ancient forest that he had read about. His mother had gotten him a book of dinosaurs that described such a scene. He could imagine volcanoes and rotting vegetation. He saw coal being mined and wondered why men would work this way. The coal seam was twelve feet high and many large slabs had fallen alongside the track. His granddad had warned him to always stay in the middle of the track. He saw the workers standing in water over their shoes. He watched them load out a cut of coal and saw how hard it was for them. His nature was such that he felt pain for these men he did not know. When they finally reached the surface he asked his grandfather, "Why do those men work where it is so scary?"

"It's for this, boy," he said, while pulling a few coins from his pocket.

Billy would come to the mine every day during the summer. His granddad had started Billy's training that year, the boy's ninth. Billy was short for his age and rather chunky. He always had a smile on his face and enjoyed everything about life and nature. It was hard for him to be serious about anything. He enjoyed playing practical jokes and the other boys looked up to him as a natural leader.

They had just walked through the gate at the mine when McGinnis spied a worker beating one of the mine's mules. McGinnis took his cane and beat the man until he collapsed. Screaming at two other men close by he had them dispose of the man outside of the gate. He then grabbed the boy telling him, "Them mules are our lifeblood, but them white niggers are a dime a dozen."

Billy was constantly being badgered by his grandfather and mother about the sins and sinners living among them. They were especially unforgiving of coal miners and their families.

"Men will try to do anything that they can get away with. You gotta remember, boy, that this ain't about them. It's about you making a livin'. You are the means that they can care for their families. If we didn't have that mine they wouldn't be employed. Most of them boys can't even read or write. If it wasn't for us, they'd starve. Don't go feelin' any sympathy for that lot."

Billy walked the rest of the way home that day in silence. He kept thinking about those men and why his grandpa was so hard on them.

Bella was standing on the porch of the two-story home waiting for Billy and Duffy. In the nine years that she had lived with her father she had watched over her son's growth like the old man watched over his mine. She was satisfied with all but his gentle manner. He was bright and had a quick wit. Even though he was short and stout, he was agile and extremely quick. The other boys his age had started hunting but she could not get him interested. His grandfather had tried many times, taking him hunting for deer and other game. He even gave the boy his own rifle. Once he had the boy stand on an outcropping of rock. The old man knew that he would get a shot from there. He watched as an eight-point buck stepped into a clearing not forty yards from his grandson. The boy did not even lift the weapon. He just watched the magnificent animal till it faded away into the trees. The granddad gave up after that.

Bella had told the boy many times the story of his father and how he was gunned down by those treacherous coal miners. She told him of that fight and its outcome. She continued to pound away at the rabble living around them, but the more that she ranted the less interest he showed. He enjoyed playing with the sons of the very rabble that she complained about.

Bella was true to her convictions. She treated the townspeople in the same manner that she suggested to her son. One day while shopping at her local grocery store the owner made the error of waiting on one of the wives of the lowly rabble before Bella. Her rant further isolated her from the citizens of Lonaconing. On this particular day there was a teacher in the store. She had no use for Bella and she said, "Lady, this isn't any kingdom and you're no queen." Bella did not even answer. She just stormed out swearing like the miners she despised. From then on, the people of Coney called her "Queen Bee".

Billy loved the town, the people, and roaming the hills nearby. One thing he did not love was the smell of the paper mill just down the road in Luke. In later years when he had entered the Army he would say he thought the whole world smelled that way. The smell was so strong it made you think the world was dead, and you were in the middle of it all.

The crash of '29 did not affect the people of Coney right away. But things gradually got worse until most of the town was out of work. People were forced to ask for charity just to feed their families. It also forced the men to seek work wherever they could find it. It drove them to McGinnis.

Duffy McGinnis despised the workers at his mine. He found them lazy and dishonest. He valued his animals above any man he knew. He did not intentionally harm any of them, but he did not go out of his way to protect anyone either. In the two years after the Depression began he had two deaths at his mine and three men disabled. There was no outcry because his mine had one of the better safety records. It was just the way things were and people accepted the risk.

Duffy was worried about the boy. No matter how he tried he could not make the boy understand that life was hard and he had to be tough. Billy only wanted to play with his friends who were part of the crowd that Duffy despised. Then one day his opinion of the boy changed. He had taken Billy to a small grocery. Duffy had seen a new kid at the store but did not give him much notice. While searching for tobacco he heard a ruckus outside. He saw Billy and the boy going at each other. The bigger boy was giving Billy the thrashing of his life. At least twenty people were standing in a circle around the two boys and most were cheering for the big boy. When Duffy got outside he yelled to Billy, "Get up, boy, nobody does that to a Storm." But the more he yelled the harder that big kid beat Billy. Again and again the big boy drove Billy to the ground, but each time Billy made it to his feet. Then with a crashing kick to Billy's balls the fight appeared over. Duffy kept yelling for Billy to get up and the crowd kept screaming for his blood. The big kid now confident as hell started strutting around with a grin that reached clean across his face. He began taking bows. Then Billy got to his feet and charged straight at the boy, with his head down. The kid was so surprised that he just stared at Billy. Billy slammed his head deep into the kid's stomach and in a fraction of a second he brought his head up violently snapping the big boy's head back with a loud crack. Like most endings, it did not end quite the way people expected. Billy heard someone yell, "Did you see that little fellow buck that big shit?" Without realizing it, Billy just got a nickname that would last the rest of his life.

CHAPTER 9
DEPRESSING DEPRESSION

Go forth to meet the shadowy future without fear and with a manly heart.

—Henry Wadsworth Longfellow, *Hyperion*

Clara stood on the porch staring at her man. He was plowing a field with their one horse. It had been ten years since she and Karl had come to Ohio and she could not have been happier. They owned seventy-five acres now and he had built her a comfortable five room home. He also kept her pregnant most of the time. They had seven little ones and she was not quite twenty-five. Gone was her girlish body and her face was already showing the lines of age. Her oldest, Tony, was just now old enough to help her and Karl. Her days were full and the work was hard, but she loved every minute.

Her only regret was the passing of her mom two years before. She looked out over the rolling hills she had come to love and wondered at it all. Oh! How she loved this place. It was very different from the steep harsh mountains where she had grown up. These hills with their many woods and open meadows were like heaven. She and Karl had their little kingdom and they knew contentment like never before. She walked over and rang the big bell letting Karl know that his lunch was ready. The sounds of the kids playing and Karl's swearing at the horse made her smile all the more.

Karl had never known a real home since he ran away after his mom had died. But here, with Clara and the kids, he had found peace. He liked the little town of Adena, Ohio. It was loaded with immigrants from all over Europe. They called America the melting pot. Well, Adena was just that. There were the Polish, Slovaks, Italians, Hungarians, Russians, Scotch, Irish, and even some from the Middle East. His children would grow up with the sons and daughters of these immigrants. He could not have been more pleased.

The town itself offered everything he and his family would ever need. There was a feed mill, hotel, theater, dry goods store, two hardware stores, four gas stations, four barber shops, four grocery stores, a drug store, two grade schools, one of which was Catholic, a high school, a doctor, a dentist, and three churches. But most important to him was the still that he kept in his barn. He enjoyed his many friends who would stop by for a drink.

When they first came to this little town Clara made it a point to attend church and to make as many friends as possible. She and Karl were quickly accepted in the community. The hardest part had been dragging Karl to church. "It's time," she would say and then he would start moaning.

He told her, "I ain't got any use for them sanctimonious bastards that run them things."

But he relented. Every Sunday he would put on his best and head to church with her and the children. That is until the Sunday that the legend of Karl began.

The Bishop had sent a letter to each of the parish priests telling them that they must do more to confront the sinners in their congregations. Wisely most of the priests had ignored the letter or had subtly applied the message, but not Adena's priest. He gave a scathing sermon about the dangers of drink and pointing right at Karl explained how the man would be going to hell. Karl waited for the priest after mass.

"Hey, priest, you and me got a problem."

The priest, small in all ways but courage, answered. "The problem is not yours and mine but yours and the bottle."

A terrible argument followed. Both men lost their tempers. No one was standing close enough to hear what was said. They all saw Karl's big fist flying. The priest made one very big mistake. He attempted to defend himself. It took four men to drag Karl off that man of God. Clara stood there looking into Karl's eyes with such fury that Karl turned away. She would say a rosary everyday the rest of her life for what Karl did that day. It was the only cloud that ever invaded their marriage. It was also the reason that Karl became the leader of the less courageous in town.

The depression had hit Karl hard. Many of the mines in the area had closed including his. The farm took care of their basic needs, but they had to have cash money. He began to look for work. His search took him to a new mine near Cadiz, Ohio, called the Nelms Mine. It had started operations in 1927, but most men shied away from it because it was so hot. To a miner, "hot" meant that it was full of methane gas. Explosions in the mines came as regularly as the seasons and the amount of methane that came from the Nelms Mine made most miners nervous. Karl had driven his old Model T to the mine and arrived near 7:00 AM. He waited with others searching for a work until about 8:00 AM. Then the mine foreman stepped out of the office to tell them that they did not need anyone.

Unknown to Karl this ritual had been going on for weeks. When the man turned to leave one of the men yelled out, "When will ya be hirn'?"

The foreman answered, "Ain't no way to tell. Just keep a comin'."

Stubborn Karl made up his mind then and there that this was where he would be working. He began a routine that would last over thirty days. Each morning he would drive to the mine, and each morning he would be told that they were not hiring. When most men went to the mine once or twice then quit, he kept coming back.

Clara asked, "Why do you keep pestering that man when he keeps telling you there's no work?"

"'Cause I aim to work there one way or the other. That mine looks to be there as long as I wanna work and maybe the boys too. I'm tired of being laid off every time we turn around."

It was May 1931 and he had been to the mine thirty-four days straight. This was it, he thought. Today I get hired or it's over. So he dressed for work and packed his bucket. He drove to the mine feeling somewhat foolish, thinking if the man sends me away with the others looking on I'll look like a fool. When he pulled up to the mine office there were only two men waiting. Within the hour the foreman appeared at the door giving his same response.

"There's no work here."

Before he could turn to enter the office Karl spoke up, "Hey."

"What you want?" answered the foreman. "And why you dressed like that?"

"Well, somebody gotta feed my family. It might as well be you."

The foreman looked at him dumbfounded. He was actually speechless. They stood staring at each other for a very long time. Finally a smile came across the foreman's face and he said, "Well, I guess you had better step in here." And that is how Karl Kamin found a job.

The depression did not hurt Clara and Karl as much as most. They had their farm and Karl had his job. The farm produced enough for most of their needs. Fresh milk, butter, meat, flour, fruit, and potatoes allowed them to eat their fill. The job gave them spending money for when it was needed. It was during this time that their oldest son Antonio, called Tony, complained about his clothes. Karl thought for some time that Tony was ashamed of him and how they lived. It began when Tony had entered school and saw what others had.

"Pa, I ain't got no good clothes to wear to church."

Karl stared at him. "What you mean? Them clothes are just fine."

"But, Pa, I ain't got no clothes without patches."

Karl answered, "As long as them clothes is clean and your shoes are shined, you're dressed up. Listen son, we are rich in some things and poor in others. But we are not beholden to any man."

"But Pa." Tony protested.

"There are them that work and them that don't. You will always have to work, Tony. Be proud of who you are. Don't worry about what you have." Karl saw the confused look on his son's face. He hoped in time that he would learn.

CHAPTER 10
HOPES AND FEARS

A woman's hopes are woven of sunbeams, a shadow annihilates them.

—George Eliot

31 DIE IN MINE-COUNTY'S WORST DISASTER

—*Cadiz Republican*, December 5, 1940

As time went on, the Kamins were blessed with five sons and three daughters. All were healthy and all made them proud. Then one April day in 1940 Clara told Karl that she was pregnant with their ninth child. They had been married eighteen years and it had been ten years since their last child was born. Karl was now fifty years old and he was beginning to feel his age. When he told his friends one yelled out, "Hey, maybe we should start calling him the bull." Karl took the teasing in stride, but it was hard to hide his pride in becoming a father again.

Just a few days before Clara told Karl about her pregnancy an event occurred that scared her to death. The Willow Grove mine in Neffs, Ohio exploded. There were seventy-two men killed in that explosion. The mine was owned by the Hanna Coal Division of Consol Coal Company and was said to be the safest and most advanced mine in the country. It was just the year before that Eleanor Roosevelt, the President's wife, had visited the mine. This was Clara's greatest fear. Her father and brothers had been killed at the Monongah No. 8 Mine in the early part of the century when she was very young. She never told Karl how she felt. But each time he went off to work she shivered with fear. The time passed quickly and as the birth of her child approached she became more apprehensive.

As they lay in bed they made a game out of their hopes for their new child. Karl saw the child as a boy and wanted him to be a doctor or lawyer. Clara would smile and rub her belly telling Karl their new daughter would be a schoolteacher or a nurse, but both were adamant that the child would never be a coal miner.

Karl did not exactly love what he did for a living but he was satisfied. Each day when he suited up at the Nelms Mine he reminded himself that few men in this large country would do what he did for a living. When he got on the cage to be lowered into the mine he would always say a little prayer asking God to allow him to return to the fresh air safely.

"Hey, Karl, why don't you talk to the mine foreman about what's going on in our section?" complained one of the men. Their work section was located in the 8 East air course. The working areas of the mine were always indicated by direction. "They don't even give us rock dust for the section," the man added.

Karl answered, "When we go out today I'll have a talk with him."

It took about 20 minutes for the men to get to the section from the shaft bottom. The mine was walking height. The coal seam was about five feet thick and the men removed two feet of rock to allow seven feet of height.

The men went to their machines and began work. Even though the foreman was carrying a bug light to check for methane the checks were made haphazardly. The bug light was officially called a flame safety lamp. With this device you could determine the amount of methane in an area and also the amount of oxygen. The Nelms Mine was extremely hot and liberated hundreds of thousands of cubic feet of methane a day. Karl knew that with winter approaching the mine was drying out. This contributed to the danger that the men faced.

"Let's wet down the section," he told the foreman.

"Later, I want you to go help on the cutting machine," the foreman answered.

Karl grumbled but did as he was told. At lunchtime the men were all complaining about the conditions of the section.

"As soon as we get outside I'll go talk to the Superintendent." Karl told them. Karl never liked working on the cutting machine because of the dust that it generated. The machine would undercut the coal using a huge cutting bar with a chain that would rip the coal from the bottom. Then the coal would be drilled and explosives used to bring it down. Then the coal was loaded onto buggies for its journey to the surface.

The foreman interrupted him again. This time he directed Karl to run the coal loading machine while the regular operator ate his lunch. The first coal buggy was loaded without incident, but when the second approached, Karl's eyes saw what his mind could not comprehend. He saw a blue flame dance and then darkness.

Karl along with thirty other men died in an instant.

The methane ignition had put the coal dust in suspension. The very air seemed to explode. Like a chimney fire the explosions came one after another until they exhausted the fuel that propelled them.

A company safety man was walking an air course between the 8 East section and the surface when a blast of air knocked him off his feet. He immediately went to a mine phone and started calling the sections. The only one that did not answer was the 8 East section. The mine was evacuated and one hundred four men surfaced without injury. One of those men was Karl's oldest son Anthony. Mine rescue teams arrived and the recovery of bodies from the doomed section began.

Clara was beginning to worry. It was getting late and her two men were not back yet. Then she saw lights coming up the lane and recognized Karl's old Model A Ford that he had recently purchased. She went out to meet them and saw that Tony had been driving. With fear in her eyes she rushed to him. "It's Pop, he's dead, Ma." Her screams filled that cool night's air. Within ten minutes she went into labor and with only her children to help her she delivered a baby boy. She named him Karl Jesse Kamin.

With the loss of Karl, Clara's life changed completely. Her first decision was to find some type of work. She knew that it was up to her to sustain her family. The coal company had paid for Karl's funeral but that was the extent of their help.

Unexpectedly a man approached her about becoming his housekeeper. He was the only man of wealth in the town. She accepted with gratitude. With that worry out of the way her next thought was of the child. The older children would have to help with him so she could work. They would all work together to survive.

CHAPTER 11
STORM CLOUDS

Young men are fitter to invent than to judge, fitter for execution than for counsel, and fitter for new projects than for settled business.

—Francis Bacon, *Of Youth and Age*

Billy "Buck" Storm was having a blast. He had just turned twenty, he was in his second year at West Virginia University and he was in love. Her name was Jamie McNabb and she was a cheerleader. They had met the year before when he made the squad on WVU's football team. He stood only 5'8" but he was built like a block of granite. They had made him a guard which had suited him just fine. He had spotted Jamie that first game and found a girl who knew her and arranged an introduction. They hit it off immediately and had been dating ever since.

College life was ideal for him. He liked the freedom, the easy atmosphere and above all he liked being away from his mother. She had turned into a very bitter woman who had never recovered from the death of her husband. It had been twenty years and she still had such hatred for those responsible that a day did not go by without her speaking of it. He was dreading going home for Thanksgiving. He planned on taking Jamie with him and he wanted the day to be great. His mother knew about the girl, and unknown to Billy, she had already begun to harbor resentment towards her. You see, she had plans for Billy. He was to be her avenging angel. He would be the instrument of that revenge.

The day arrived and as they pulled into the drive of Billy's home the first thing he saw was his grandfather. Billy idolized the tough old bird. Duffy McGinnis tried mighty hard to make Billy a no nonsense man but the boy was too easygoing. In fact the only thing the old man thought Billy was serious about was this girl.

"Hi, Grandpa, I want you to meet Jamie." Billy said almost breathlessly.

A little stiffly McGinnis answered. "It's nice to meet ya young lady."

"Where's Ma?" Billy asked.

"She's checking on the bird." The old man answered.

When they went inside they found Billy's mom giving the cook hell. Billy knew better than to ask what had happened. Some imaginary offense that the cook had been accused of, he supposed. When he finally got her attention, he walked over to her with Jamie, hand in hand.

"This is Jamie." He said.

Without even offering the girl her hand she answered. "Well, William, she is pretty enough." Bella's inhospitable ways even made her father angry.

He spoke up quickly, "We welcome you, young lady, into our house."

They made it through dinner without a word being said. When they had adjourned to the living room Billy's grandfather spoke up.

"Boy, I don't want you getting involved with the Army. There's war coming and we got a business to run. I seen it in the last war. Miners and those who run the mines were sorely needed."

"But, Grandpa, if war comes I want to go." He answered.

His grandpa stared at him hard. "I served in the Army and I know how them officers waste men. Like they were no more account than a sack of beans. Now you heard me, that ends it."

With his mother so hostile and his grandfather so adamant they ended their unpleasant visit.

When they got to the car Billy said, "Jamie I'm so sorry for how they treated you."

"It's you that I feel sorry for, Billy. You have to suffer through such unpleasantness all the time." Then she cried.

Jamie and his mother were the only people that still called him Billy. He preferred Buck. He decided that from that day forward Buck it would be.

CHAPTER 12
WAR'S UNENDING DESTRUCTION

War is as much a punishment for the punisher as to the sufferer.

—Thomas Jefferson, Letter, 1794

ELEMENTS OF THE 85TH INFANTRY DIVISION AND THE 10TH MOUNTAIN DIVISION SECURE VERONA

—*The Po Valley Campaign*, April 26, 1945

The war that Buck's grandfather worried over came with a vengeance on the 7th of December. He was home on that Sunday when the bulletins came across the radio. Without even excusing himself Buck got into his car and drove to Morgantown. He saw Jamie and told her his intentions. The following morning William Buck Storm enlisted in the United States Army.

It did not take Buck long to find out that he hated the Army. The enlisted men were treated no better than slaves. He quickly decided that he would become an officer if that were possible. When the brass found out that he had nearly two years of college he was picked for Officers Candidate School. He graduated first in his class.

The years dragged on slowly. He could not believe that three years had passed since he had enlisted. He still had not left the country. He had volunteered for a combat assignment so many times that he had lost track. This problem started at the end of Officers Candidate School. He had casually mentioned that he was a terrific skier. He was overheard by a major who had been assigned the duty of finding instructors for a new training command. They were to teach skiing and rock climbing to various members of the armed forces and the Office of Strategic Services, our spies. Buck was immediately assigned to the training command.

Jamie and he remained close and he complained regularly of the injustice done to him. Jamie had remained at WVU. She graduated with the hope that he would never see combat. She also longed to marry him but he refused to discuss this with her until the war ended.

In late 1944 Buck's wish was granted with the formation of the 10th Mountain Division. He was assigned a rifle company in one of the newly formed battalions. Captain William Buck Storm was finally getting his wish and was heading off to war. The Division arrived in Italy and saw combat in January of 1945. Like all men who fantasize about war, the reality can be horrific. Buck was no exception. In his first month of combat his company lost seventy-five men either wounded or killed. By the end of February he had the eyes and manner of a veteran. He would give all he had to be away from this place. He was constantly cold, wet, and downright miserable. He heard from Jamie regularly but he quit writing. He truly believed he would never see her again.

Buck was in a daze. He thought of yesterday's fight and started to shake. The company was advancing on yet another village, one they thought had been abandoned. His company was in the lead. As they entered the town three machine guns opened up cutting down a third of his force. The men were immobilized. Without thinking Buck yelled for covering fire and attacked the guns alone. The next five minutes were a blur. The gun that he focused his attack on jammed giving him time and saving his life. He eliminated the two soldiers manning the gun and now he had the second gun flanked. In quick succession he destroyed the remaining guns. His men were able to secure the town without any further casualties. Buck's actions that day were observed by his battalion commander. The commander put Buck in for a Silver Star.

Of all the men Buck served with he was closest to his company's First Sergeant, Albert Kominski. They had been together since Buck was assigned as a ski instructor. Kominski was from Shinnston, West Virginia. He was two years older than Buck and contrary to Army regulations they spent a lot of off-duty time together.

It was the twenty-sixth of April and all could sense that the war was close to being over. Everyone wanted to make sure that they were alive to see that end. That included Buck.

"Hey, Buck," Ski called.

"Yeah, what is it?" Buck answered through half open eyes. He was filthy, tired, and angry.

"A change of plans, Battalion wants us to do a recon of that town before they move up." Ski saw that his friend was still half asleep.

"What, the whole company?" He answered with astonishment.

"No, just a squad. Who do you want should go?"

Buck thought for a long moment. He did not want to

expose any of the men this late in the game. Finally he said, "Get me Lt. Amos!"

Amos walked into the burned out shack that the company was using for a command post. "You wanted me, Sir?"

Buck looked the man in the eyes and answered. "Yeah, I want you to take command of the company until I return."

"What the hell you doing, Buck?" Ski exclaimed.

"That's what the hell you doing, Sir." Buck answered with a grin.

He turned to Amos, "I'm taking out your first squad."

Ski spoke up, "You ain't goin' nowhere without me, Sir." He drug out the last word so long that even Amos laughed, until he got a hard look from Storm.

Buck pulled Ski off to the side but before he could say anything, Ski volunteered. "Listen, Buck, you don't want me sitting back here worrying myself sick. Besides I would rather go than send one of them kids."

Buck allowed his stern gaze to soften. "What the hell. Ain't no one gonna believe that a company commander and his first sergeant went out on a patrol."

Within thirty minutes they were approaching their objective. Checking out the town with his field glasses he said, "Do you know what town that is, Ski?" Ski just shook his head no. "It's Verona, the city of tragic love."

"What the hell is that?" Ski answered.

"Hell, boy, didn't you ever read Shakespeare? That's the place where Romeo and Juliet bit the dust."

"I heard of them but I didn't know this was the place. Anyway, who gives a shit?" Ski blurted out.

"Hell, Ski, you'll be able to tell your grandkids about this place. Now let's get movin'."

They entered the town that reminded Buck of a stone

quarry. The people were lucky if one in ten houses was standing. The artillery did a job on this place, he thought. Then it happened. Ski was about ten yards ahead and to Buck's left when a shot rang out. Everyone hit the dirt and then Buck noticed that Ski was lying in the open. He ran to his side just as another shot sounded. The squad provided covering fire while Buck pulled Ski to safety. Buck rolled Ski onto his back and saw with horror that he had been shot right between the eyes. Buck knelt there for a moment and a rage filled him like he had never known.

He kicked the door in of a building that would allow him to use its cover to get at that sniper. He aimed to kill that son-of-a-bitch. He was out of his head screaming when he charged into that building and with the firing going on outside he did not even realize it. He walked through one room and entered another. Then the firing died down and he heard a noise behind him. He turned and fired, spraying the room with his Thompson submachine gun. Lying not more than ten feet from him were the bullet-riddled bodies of a young boy and a young girl. They could not have been more than ten years old.

The noise that Buck heard was not the children but debris that had shifted. They did not have time to make a sound when the shots rang out. Buck stared at what he had done and tears welled up in his eyes. He ran from that building. His men screamed for him to get down but he could not hear them. All he saw was those children. All he heard was the sound of his own demons. A mortar shell landed within a few yards of him, mercifully flooding his mind with darkness.

CHAPTER 13
LOST LOVE, LOST LIFE

Everyone can master a grief but he that has it.

—William Shakespeare, *Much Ado about Nothing*, Act III, Sc. 2

The war was over in Europe. Jamie could have cried with relief. Her darling Billy would be safe and would be home soon. She had not heard from him in weeks but she was sure he was OK or someone would have told her. Then she received a call. It was not Billy's mother but his grandfather who called.

"Miss McNabb, this is Billy's granddad. I wanted to let you know that he was injured and is being sent to Walter Reed Hospital in Washington. They said he would arrive tomorrow."

Distraught, she asked. "How bad is he, sir?"

"We don't know. That is all that we were told."

"Thank you for letting me know," she added.

The old man's final comment was, "Don't go a worrin'. That boy is tough as hell."

She packed a few things and caught the evening train to Washington. The beautiful spring evening could not lift her spirits. She kept imagining what she would find. She thought he could be crippled or worse. She made up her mind that what ever she found, her love and his would carry them through.

Buck was laying in bed just staring out the window. He had barely said a word since he awoke in a field hospital, the first of May. There was celebration all around him because the word had just come down that the war was over. He was told his wounds were serious but the doctors expected him to make a full recovery. They did say he might have a slight limp. What the doctors did not know was that Buck wanted to die. He would barely eat. He would not do much of anything. He tried to force himself to stay awake. Each time he shut his eyes he could see those beautiful children ripped to bits by his bullets.

It was nearly noon when a nurse came in announcing that he had visitors. His mother, grandfather, and Jamie were waiting to see him.

"Ask my grandfather to come in, please."

When his grandfather stepped in, Buck said, "Tell 'em that I don't want to see anyone now. Will ya, Grandpa? I can't talk right now, not even to you."

"What's a matter, boy?" His granddad asked.

Buck screamed. "Just leave me alone!"

When Duffy told the women what Buck wanted both started to argue.

Duffy said, "Let's give him time."

Jamie had made up her mind that she would talk to Buck before the day was out, so had his mother. Two hours later she stood outside of his room debating whether to enter or not. She finally mustered enough courage and opened the door. He was in bed staring out the window and did not hear her come in. She was shocked at how he appeared. He had lost a great amount of weight. He had aged twenty years and he wore a scowl that frightened her.

She yelled in anguish, "Billy."

He turned to her not with love but indifference. "I said I didn't want to talk to anyone. Please leave, Jamie." He turned and continued to stare out the window. She started to say something but thought better of it. She finally turned and walked away not knowing that this would be the last time that she would ever see William Buck Storm.

CHAPTER 14
JESSE'S WORLD

Ah! Happy Years! Once more who would not be a boy!

—Lord Bryon, *Childe Harold*

It was 1950 and Karl Jesse Kamin was like a wild pup running loose in a world of wonders. He split his time between his mom's farm and his oldest brother Tony's home in New Town, Ohio. There was an eighteen year difference between the brothers. Tony felt more like Jesse's father than a brother. After the explosion that had killed their father, Tony had not returned to the Nelms Mine. He had gotten a job at the Dunglen Mine of Hanna Coal Company. He also got himself a wife. They had two children and lived in a company house in New Town. Tony's oldest boy also named Tony was two years younger than Jesse and the boys were becoming fast friends. They spent their days playing on the gob piles that surrounded the town. The mine produced so much waste that the gob, a mixture of coal and rock, was enormous. There was a big old red dog pile on one end of town. The gob, coal and rock, burned and created this mixture that was used on roads and driveways. The boys explored it all. Tony kept telling them to stay off that red dog because it was constantly smoking and smoldering. Hell, that pile had even exploded ten years earlier. Nobody had gotten hurt, thank God.

Tony's house had four rooms: two bedrooms, a kitchen, and a living room. They had a hand pump at the kitchen sink and a two-hole outhouse on the back porch about ten feet away from that sink. The boys loved to watch the honey dippers come and empty the two fifty-gallon drums under the holes. The house had a coal stove in the basement where Tony's wife did all her cooking. There were also fifty-gallon drums on two corners of the house for catching rain water from the downspouts. In the front of the house was a white picket fence. Well, it was supposed to be white, but with all the trains passing through no one could tell.

There was so much soot in the air that the houses and fences looked more like a dingy gray than white. There was a huge drainage ditch between the road and the picket fence with a foot bridge. The boys just loved playing in that ditch. Money was tight but they made do. The house cost Tony fifteen dollars a month rent. With no running water, Tony took the boys to the mine bath house for showers once a week. That was a real treat.

Tony had started calling his brother "Jesse" to the chagrin of his mom soon after his father's death. But the name stuck, and to everyone but Tony's mother the boy was Jesse. Jesse was a kid who just would not sit still. When they took him to church someone would end up walking out with him. When he started school, the same complaints came from there. Just the other day Tony heard Jesse say, "I want it. I want it bad. I just don't know what it is." That pretty much summed up Jesse. He could not stick to anything for more than a few minutes. He was not stupid, but if it did not interest him it was like driving a spike through a steel wall. You just were not going to get in.

Between the town and the farm Jesse kept busy. He was not much for work, but you sure could count on him when play was involved. On his tenth Christmas Tony bought him and little Tony BB guns. The boys were given the normal cautions and they were let go. The guns were used on cans, bottles, and a couple of windows. With unlimited freedom the two explored their world. As long as they showed up for meals and before dark they were free to do whatever their hearts desired.

In the spring Jesse and little Tony were playing with their guns and got the brainy idea of playing war. They went to the creek and each took up position on one of the two railroad bridge abutments that supported the bridge. They began to fire at each other and within a few minutes Jesse stuck his head out from behind his hiding place and was struck with a BB. With tears in his eyes and anger in his heart he shouted and Tony stepped out to see what the problem was and Jesse fired. He saw Tony throw his gun into the creek screaming and running towards the town. Jesse caught him in the ditch in front of Tony's home. When he rolled Tony over he saw immediately what had happened. Jesse had shot out one side of the boy's glasses. When he had assured himself that Tony was not hurt, he said, "Don't tell your folks what happened. They won't let us play together again. Just say that you fell and broke your glasses on a rock." The boys did just that. Carrying their guns they told the lie and to their surprise they were believed.

Jesse learned a valuable lesson with the guns. It made him sick thinking of what could have happened to Tony. If Jesse ever had a prayer it was to never hurt anyone by what he did or did not do.

CHAPTER 15
GRANDPA'S ULTIMATUM

What can't be cured must be endured.

—English Proverb

Buck Storm sat in the dark room with a bottle of whiskey. He had been home for eight months and had been drunk most of the time. No one could talk to him. Jamie had called several times but he had refused to talk with her. Her last attempt to contact him ended with him screaming "leave me the fuck alone!" In his bleary state all he could see was the two children lying dead by his hand. His mind was becoming so warped that he began treating everyone with contempt. The once jolly young man became a disgusting, grotesque hermit. One cold winter morning a knock on his door produced the normal scathing response when to Buck's surprise the door was knocked from its hinges and there stood his grandfather.

"Boy, it's time that you got off your ass. I don't know what happened to you over there and I don't wanna know."

Buck stared at him with hatred. "Leave me alone. You don't have any idea what I've been through."

His grandfather far from cowed came back with, "What the hell do you think you are, a Democrat? The only thing you're entitled to in this life boy is air to breathe. You got work to do and this ends today." With that he jerked the bottle from Buck's hand and threw it against the wall. Glass flew in a hundred directions. He then went to the windows and pulled back the drapes flooding the room with light. "You got one hour to get your ass down them stairs and ready for work. If you don't, the next time I come in here I'll have help, and I guarantee you won't like it." With that he stormed from the room.

CHAPTER 16
WHAT CAN I DO?

The more haste ever the worst speed.

—Charles Churchill

Jesse began his high school years in much the same way as grade school. He had very little interest and no desire to accomplish anything. He did like football. Even at this he failed. He had the ability but he would not learn the plays. He was not about to study anything. Even when his nephew, Tony Jr., became a star running back Jesse would not change. He did not put much effort into anything including what he loved. Sure he would get all excited each Friday night when it was time for the games. He really liked how the school band would start out from the American Legion. It was about a quarter mile from the football field. They played great marching songs as they went. The sound echoed throughout the valley. The townspeople would fall in behind the band and the whole procession would march to the field.

Jesse was in love with his town, from its brick lined streets to its dozen beer joints. He liked its people. The men were tough and did not take anything from anybody. They were a mixture of coal miners, mill workers, and railroad men. The women for the most part were as tough as their men. These were the children and grandchildren of the people who built this great country. For all the good that he saw in his town, he was still being raised in a sea of hatred. That

73

hatred was directed at the big shots who ran the mines, the mills and the government. Most of that hate he learned at home. His mother had never forgiven those responsible for his father's death. She lectured Jesse every night. "Them men destroyed your daddy and many others. Don't you forget it. Some day you will be in a position to right some of them wrongs. Never forget where you come from, boy." Jesse would always shake his head and agree with every word she said. The hardest thing to take was the ritual at every suppertime. In their dining room on one wall hung a picture of Franklin Delano Roosevelt and across from him hung the picture of John L. Lewis. Lewis was the president of the United Mine Workers of America. Each night he had to join her in praying to those two men. One saved the country and the other saved the coal miner, she would say. Jesse had made up his mind that he would never set foot in a mine, even if his mother tried to force him. He began spending more time at his brother Tony's house.

CHAPTER 17
THE MASTER

He who commits injustice is ever made more wretched than he who suffers it.

—Plato

Buck Storm had found his purpose in life. Within a week of his grandfather ordering him from his room he had found coal mining. He attacked the coal as if it were his enemy. He could outload any two men, when it came to filling a coal car. His strength returned in a rage but he remained one of the most bitter and mean men in Lonaconing, Maryland. The mines abruptly became his when his grandfather died, bellowing at one of his workers. Buck now became what no one would have suspected: a man as mean as his grandfather. He treated men and women alike. He did not respect anyone or anything. Even his mother shied away from him when he turned those bitter eyes towards her. She had raised him to exact her revenge on miners whom she blamed for her husband's death. But even she was not prepared for his savage ways.

In 1957 a bitter recession enveloped the nation. Times were hard for everybody, including small business owners. Buck always treated his men like slaves. If one whined within his hearing, he promptly fired him. There was no such thing as benefits at his mine. If a worker got hurt and could not continue he got a week's pay and that was it. One day two men showed up in town. They belonged to the United Mine

Workers of America and were there to organize the men along Georges Creek. These were the coalfields that stretched from Frostburg to Westernport, Maryland.

Coal was mined in the two most Western counties of Maryland, Garrett and Allegheny. There were mines all along the Georges Creek, which took its name from an Indian who hunted that area long ago. The men made the mistake of targeting Storm's mine. They met with many of the workers and heard the horrifying descriptions of the conditions that they worked under. One of the organizers was a black man named Booker T. Katts. He told the men stories of the bitter coal wars in West Virginia that his father had participated in and how the men united to protect themselves. But each time the men would tell him, "You ain't been up against anyone like Storm." Eventually word of what was happening got back to Storm. Storm had some of his associates confront the Union workers late one evening, as they were returning to their hotel.

Directing his words to Katts, one yelled out, "Hey, boy, I'll have a word with you." Katts was startled by the appearance of the four hooded men. Before he and his companion could respond to the threat, they were seized by the men. The men were large and strong. Katts, his words laced with fear, asked. "What do you want?"

"There ain't gonna be no more Union trash throwed at Georges Creek. You got it?" One said.

Katts started to laugh but was cut short. "Listen, nigger, you and this other shit are leaving now." The two Union men were beaten so badly that they would spend months in the hospital. When they were released, the Union tried to bring charges against

Storm but he had an alibi that would stand like steel. Finally the incident faded away and was forgotten. Never would the Union be allowed into Georges Creek.

CHAPTER 18
CHOICELESS LIFE

How few our real wants and how vast our imaginary ones!

—Johann Kaspar Lavater

Tony Jr. asked, "What ya gonna do when you graduate?"

Jesse thought for a minute. "I guess I'll hang out with you for at least the summer."

Tony laughed. "Grandma sure ain't gonna like that."

"We just won't tell her. Anyway, I won't be eighteen until November. You and I can put up hay this summer. There ain't a farmer around here that don't need help. Ma wants me to get your pa to help me get a job at Hanna Coal. I keep telling her that I don't want it. I ain't going into no coal mine." Jesse thought that he might go into the Army or something. He wanted to see the world. He would not work in darkness the rest of his life.

The summer was going along nicely until Jesse met Connie. She was blond, she was pretty, and she lit up like a bonfire every time he came around. They were the same age but she was from Dillonvale. In high school they would not have given each other a glance. The two schools, Dillonvale and Adena, were rivals in everything. In fact, until that summer they had no idea that the other existed. They had met by accident. She had taken a job for the summer at an ice cream stand near Harrisville. It sat along Route 250 about five miles from Adena. One day Tony and Jesse showed up for some great custard ice cream. Jesse got more than he dreamed. One look at Connie in that tight fitting blouse was all that it took.

For the remainder of the summer Jesse spent more time at the ice cream stand than he did working. Within a couple of weeks he got up enough nerve to ask her out. From then on there was no keeping them apart. The only available car that Jesse had was his mom's old Model A. His father had bought it the year before he was born. Jesse was embarrassed every time he drove it. He did not realize that Connie could care less about cars. The only thing that interested her was him. But like most seventeen year old boys he had two things on his mind and one of them was cars. He went to the one person he could talk to. He went to his nephew.

"Tony, what should I do? I don't make enough money putting up hay to buy a car. What do you think?"

Tony was about to laugh when he realized that Jesse was serious. "I think you only got one choice. Yeah, you got to get a job. You sure as hell don't want to go into the Army. You would have money, but you would never see her. I think you should talk to Pop. See if he can get you into the mine."

Jesse looked stunned. "I don't want to work in no mine."

"Then try the steel mill. You ain't got much choice." Tony stared at his uncle who looked like a whipped puppy.

Jesse thought for a moment. "I got time. I don't turn eighteen until November. You know, Tony, I sure wish I was back in school with you. I don't much like thinking about going to work for the rest of my life."

"Well, Uncle Jess, what did you expect? You only

have three choices. You can't go to school. You was lucky to get out of high school. You won't go in the Army. That leaves the mills or the mines."

For days Jesse pondered his choices. He came to the same conclusions that Tony had. He just did not have any choices. For the next six weeks he began looking around for work. No one was hiring. He checked the mills, the railroad, the strip mines, and even looked into some stores in Wheeling, West Virginia. He got the same story at each place. "Times are hard. Why don't you go to school and learn a trade?" "I hate school" was his only reply. He began to get desperate. As much as he hated to, he would have to go to big Tony.

"I need you to help me get a job, Tony. I think I could be a good coal miner." He said half heartedly.

"I'm sorry, kid, but the company ain't hirin'."

"But you said I ought to be a coal miner like Pa."

Tony looked at him with pity. "This recession has cut into their coal sales real bad. Hell, we're only working two days a week."

Jesse's visions of that car were vanishing right before his eyes. "What can I do, Tony?"

"Well, Jess, if you want to work, you're gonna have to go to one of the big cities to find it. Maybe Cleveland or Pittsburgh will have a job for you." Seeing those sad eyes, he added, "What the hell you worrying about, Jess? You got a warm place to sleep and all the food you need. Mom sure as hell won't kick you out. And you know that you are always welcome here."

Jesse could not tell his brother that he was in love and needed a car to impress his girl. He thanked him and took off searching for young Tony. He never did find Tony that day but he ended up in Cadiz, Ohio, driving right past the Y&O shaft mine where his father had been killed. He was warned by his brother and mother to stay away from that mine. "That is one place that you never want to work," they told him. He turned around and drove to the mine office. He felt like a prisoner going to the gallows. Each step was carrying him to his destiny and he was powerless to prevent it. He walked into the mine office and announced that he was looking for a job. It just happened that he was addressing the mine superintendent. "What's your name, boy?"

Jesse quickly answered, "Jesse Kamin, sir."

"You any relation to Karl Kamin?" The superintendent asked.

"Yeah, he was my pa," said Jesse.

Staring at Jesse the man finally added, "You think you can handle this kind of work?"

"I can do anything if you show me." Jesse blurted out.

"Tell you what, kid, I'm gonna take a chance. You come back here tomorrow ready to go to work. Be here by 7:30 AM."

Jesse's eyes were about ready to pop out of his head. "I'll be here," he said with a big grin.

As the boy left another man approached the superintendent. "What the hell did you do that for? We don't need anymore men."

The superintendent stared after the boy and answered. "His pa was a friend of mine. I owe him."

CHAPTER 19
THE SHIFT

Leap out of the frying pan into the fire.

—Miguel de Cervantes, *Don Quixote*

"Hey, kid, this way." The foreman led the boy into the mine bath house. The screen door opened with a twang as the spring expanded. The tension on that spring was as tight as a banjo string. When the man let go of the door, it closed with a loud crack. The boy jumped straight into the air. He felt as tight as that spring. He was being pulled into who knows what and he felt as anxious as he did on his first date.

The room they entered was a good one hundred feet long and at least fifty feet wide. There were eight rows of benches stretching the entire length of the room. Each bench was against a pipe frame that was chest high. Every two feet a chain was hooked to the pipe. The chains were threaded through a pulley that was attached to the twenty foot high ceiling. Just below the pulley hung a basket with four huge metal hooks suspended from it. A basket was assigned to every miner. At the start of the shift, they would lower the basket which had all their clothes for work. These included their mine belt, hard hat, and tools. They would then raise the basket with their street clothes to the ceiling. Having the baskets suspended in such a manner allowed the wet or damp clothes to dry before they were needed again.

The young boy would never forget the smell of that place. The room reeked of the pungent odor of sweat. He could also smell oil which saturated most of the clothes. The place reminded him of his high school locker room. The locker room's smell, at times, was overpowering but this place was distinctive. The coal dust added to that unique smell. He hoped that he would get used to it.

The boy knew that the man he followed was the top foreman at the mine. His name was Jake and he answered directly to the superintendent. Jake had been working in the mines for twenty-five years and had never finished high school. He was not a big man but the others jumped when he hollered.

"Hey, Steve, this kid will be on your crew. Listen to him, boy, and you'll do okay."

"You got it, boss," Steve Gower replied. Gower was the exact opposite of Jake. He was well over six feet and weighed at least two hundred and fifty pounds. He also had a smile on his face most of the time. One could not say that about Jake.

As he watched the mine foreman leave, the boy thought, he's got some nerve calling me a kid. I'm eighteen years old and I got me a job that pays as much as any old man here. I deserve better than that. I'll bet that son-of-a-bitch is at least forty years old. Yeah, that old bastard got some nerve.

Steve interrupted his thoughts, "Take that basket right there. You got about thirty minutes to get dressed. See me when you're done."

A man with a cloth bag draped over his shoulder bumped into the boy. He nearly knocked him down. "What's your name, kid?" The man asked. This fellow was truly interesting. He was smoking a pipe that was held in place by the only tooth in his head. His face was weathered like leather. He was a wiry little fellow who did not seem very friendly.

The boy spoke up, "I'm Jesse Kamin."

"You any relation to Karl?"

"Yeah, he was my dad."

"My name is Homer Stemkowski. Your pa and I worked together for years."

Jesse had never seen this man before, but he knew that there were over five hundred men employed at this mine. The superintendent had told him that when he came looking for a job. He had also told Jesse that he was the first person that they had hired in years. The recession of 1957 had slowed down all the businesses in the country. It was hard to believe that it was 1958 and he had found a job without much effort.

Jesse started to unpack the bag that his mother had fixed for him. It contained a set of wool socks, long johns, blue jeans, flannel shirt, bib overhauls, and a lined denim jacket. He also found a towel and wash cloth. It did not make sense. It was November, but big Tony said he would need them. Jesse was inclined not to put on the long johns.

Homer saw what he was about to do and said, "Boy, you better put on all them clothes. You're going to need them."

Jesse did not even bother to answer. He just shrugged his shoulders and started to dress. He wondered how he would ever be able to work. By the time he had his steel-toed boots, hard hat, and mine belt on, he felt like an Eskimo dressed for winter. He could hardly move. Jesse thought that being five feet eight and only weighing one hundred and twenty pounds was small until now. With all that gear, he had to weigh at least one hundred and forty pounds.

Jesse walked outside searching for Steve Gower. It was nearly sixty degrees and he was really sweating. He found Gower in the lamp room. This was where all the cap lamps were kept. The man who took care of this place had the job everyone wanted. He had heard his brother say that several times.

Gower said, "Kid, each shift you work you'll hang your tag on that board when you pick up your light. At the end of your shift, you will return the lamp here and pick up your tag. Remember to put the light on charge." The tag that Gower mentioned was a brass tag with Jesse's check number on it. The number was 1811. Jesse had an identical tag riveted to his mine belt. Jesse's brother had explained that this was the system used to determine who was in the mine. They also used the tags to identify the dead in mine fires and explosions. The tag was indestructible.

Jesse felt comical with the get up that he was wearing, but he was no different than the rest of the men. They were all smoking their last minute cigarettes, pipes, and cigars. He saw the guys stashing their smoking stuff in a small shack near the hoist. He remembered that the men were not supposed to be smoking underground. He started to daydream about the new car that he was going to buy with his first paycheck. All of a sudden, a heavy hand came down on his shoulder jarring him back into reality.

"Where in the hell is your lunch bucket?" Steve Gower was not smiling this time.

"I left it in the car."

"Go get it. Homer, you wait for him."

Homer Stemkowski glared at Gower. "Babysitting, at my age. Can you imagine that?"

The other men had heard the exchange and they laughed. To Jesse, the laughter was like being back in school and doing something stupid. He ran as fast as he could to the parking lot and retrieved his bucket. Even the bucket looked dumb. It was round. It was made up of three parts. The bottom contained about a half gallon of water. The top part held his dinner and it fit inside a flange on the bottom container, and then a lid. His brother had told him that it was made in that manner so that the miners would have water with them if they were ever trapped. He ran all the way back to the hoist cage.

Homer Stemkowski was the only one left outside by the time Jesse got back. Homer never said a word. He just slid the metal gate up out of the way and entered the cage. Jesse followed him. Homer pushed up on a metal object hanging to the side of the shaft housing. This was a vacuum whistle that signaled the hoist man to drop the cage. The cage was a four-sided affair that held twenty men. The inside top had metal rungs that the men held on to. The front and rear were open to allow people to come and go. The floor was a mixture of heavy wood and rail. This allowed men, equipment, and supplies to use the cage. The shaft that they were in was five hundred fifty feet deep. It had two compartments. On one side the coal was brought out in skips. These were huge buckets. The cage Jesse was on was used to transport everything but coal. A hoist man controlled both the cage and the skips. Jesse had heard stories about this but the ride was his first time into an underground mine. He was not prepared for the beating and banging that the cage took. He was sweating more than ever, but this time it had nothing to do with the heat. The mine had been opened in the summer of 1927. Over time, the shaft had shifted causing the cage to follow a less than straight drop to the bottom.

The sight that Jesse beheld as he exited the cage was far different than he expected. They first entered a room with huge metal doors. As the door shut behind them, Jesse's ears plugged. As Homer opened the second door Jesse's ears popped.

"This is an air lock," Homer told him. "Keep's the air in the mine at a constant speed. Without it, you couldn't control the air where coal is being mined." Jesse did not quite understand but shook his head as if he did.

When they stepped from the airlock, Jesse saw another sight that amazed him. The entire mine was white. A white dust had been sprayed on everything.

"That's called rock dust," Homer explained.

Jesse saw large electrical boxes and wires hanging everywhere. He also saw railroad tracks that seemed to go in every direction. He stayed close to Homer. They had not gone twenty feet and he felt lost. He started to feel scared. Then he saw Steve Gower. Gower was talking to several men giving orders to each.

"Well, it's about time." Gower said. "Hop on in. Don't wait for an invitation." He was pointing to a dozen rail cars that normally hauled coal. They could hold four men each. Jesse followed Homer into one. The string of cars was being pulled by what Homer called a motor. It had four railroad wheels called trucks. The contraption was powered by electricity that was fed by direct current. A pole extended from the machine to a trolley wire. A metal skid plate connected to the trolley feeding power to the electrical motors that ran the machine. When the motor operator put the pole on the trolley wire, sparks showered everywhere. As the motor began to move, the slack was pulled from each car's coupler with a bang.

"Keep your head down, kid!" Homer shouted.

Jesse felt every joint in the rails. Each jar made Jesse want to cry out. Those cars did not have springs and that ride was painful. He was mesmerized by fear and anticipation. As uncomfortable as he was, he had to marvel at this new world. At times, the roof was only inches above the mine car. Then they would break into a cavern that was twenty feet high. And then they shot right back into a low place. They seemed to be flying but they were not going any faster than ten miles per hour. He caught glimpses of parked equipment that he could not identify. Every now and then he heard someone yell over a mine phone that they passed. He thought how lucky he was to be able to get a job like this. He could not wait until all his friends found out. He knew that there were not many who had the guts to work down here.

"Now you're going to appreciate those clothes." Homer yelled.

All of a sudden, the temperature fell over thirty degrees. Jesse could not believe how cold it was.

"What happened?" He asked.

"We just passed an air shaft. You can't tell from our ride but there's over two hundred and fifty thousand cubic feet of air moving in this entry, eh, the tunnel you're in. That's a lot of air in a space that's only fifteen feet wide and six feet high." It surprised Jesse how loud that he had to talk just to be heard.

The ride lasted over fifty minutes. They rode the remainder of the way in silence. Jesse had a million questions but Homer did not seem interested in talking. Everywhere that he looked was something new and unusual. Jesse saw belt lines for hauling the coal, rail tracks going everywhere, and supplies that were dumped in the holes alongside the track. There were cement blocks stacked ten high. He saw bundles of what he knew to be mine bolts. His brother used these for tomato stakes in his garden. He saw stacks and stacks of pipe that he guessed were for water lines. This world was like no other that he could imagine. Jesse marveled at this place. It should have been coal black but it was as white as snow. Everything that he had seen was covered with that white stuff. As they continued their journey, Jesse was aware that twice they came to a stop and switched off the tracks they were on. Those changes in direction had him so lost that he could never hope to find his way out without help. Everything looked the same in this place.

Again, they came to a stop. "We're turning into our section. It's called 4 Right. This track we've been on is called 15 West. There are five sections off this track. This is number four. That's why they call it 4 Right." Jesse was glad that Homer explained that. It had saved him from asking. He even understood the explanation.

There were two big wooden doors about twenty feet apart on the track entering the section. As they slowly passed through these doors, Jesse saw men holding them open. Before Jesse could ask, Homer explained. "This is an airlock. It's like what we went through on the bottom." He saw the confused look on the boy's face. "You know, where we got off the cage?"

"Oh, yeah, sure." Then to Jesse's surprise, they started down one of the steepest hills that he could imagine. He had the same feeling that he experienced on a roller coaster even though they were going pretty slowly. He never dreamed that anything like this existed so deep under the ground. They must have traveled over a thousand feet before they began to level off. "I didn't know that they had hills in here, Mr. Stemkowski?"

"Just call me Homer, boy," he said eyeing the kid like an insect. "What the hell did you expect? However that coal lays is how the bottom lays. It can go any which way. It can be level, it can drop, it can climb, and there can be steep slopes left or right. You never know until you pull the coal."

Everyone started to exit the cars. Jesse followed Homer to the miners' dinner hole. Homer motioned for him to sit on a bench. "We wait here until the boss checks the faces."

"What's that, Homer?"

"Didn't anyone tell you anything?"

"They told me stories but not about this stuff."

"Well, Gower is checking for gas and to make sure we got enough air to mine. He is also writing down where all the equipment is so he can tell us what to do. While he is off doing that, we usually have a sandwich."

It was then that Jesse started to notice the smells. Decaying wood was the first thing that came to mind. He saw posts here and there. They were holding up the roof. There was the smell of hot rubber. He had stepped on a bunch of cables as he exited the mine car. It reminded him of spaghetti. He walked over and put his hand on the cables. They were hot to the touch. He could see dust in the air. It had a smell much like being in a sawmill but sweeter and muskier. This must be the smell of the raw coal, he thought. It was about that time that Gower returned. He began giving orders to everyone. He finally got to Homer and Jesse. "Homer, you take care of utility and take the kid with you. Four and five need posted. Clean and dust six and seven."

"Aw shit, Steve, I don't need any help."

"You heard what I said. Now get moving."

"Okay, dammit." Turning to Jesse he said, "Leave your coat and bucket here." Jesse obediently followed Homer through the maze of tunnels. "Boy, I want you to listen. I ain't going to repeat myself. There is seven entries that we are driving on this section." Jesse's blank stare caused Homer to grit his tooth. "So you can understand, let's just call them tunnels. Between each tunnel we leave a block of coal that is at least fifty feet by fifty feet. Them's called pillars. They support the roof. Every fifty feet we cut through that solid block of coal. These cuts are called crosscuts. They are done at angles of ninety degrees or forty-five degrees. This allows us to keep air at the face, you know, where the coal is being mined. It also allows the equipment to move across the section."

"I'm lost already, Homer. How do you find your way around in here?"

"It's easy. You can tell if you are standing in an entry by looking. The entries run the entire length of the section. If you are standing in a crosscut, it only breaks through into another entry and they are staggered. Now look. If you are standing facing the coal face, the fresh air is coming in on the right side of the section. The air is leaving the left side of the section. Always use the air, boy. It is either hitting you in the face or in the ass. Our dinner hole is in the number four entry. That is the track entry. We separate the air with cement walls. They are built in the crosscuts and are called stoppings. One entry of fresh air is called intake and one of bad air is called return. All the other entries are called neutral entries. The belt entry for hauling the coal out is in number five. It's simple."

Jesse was more confused than ever. It was like being in a strange country where they did not even speak English. He thought he would never understand or remember all this stuff.

"Come on, kid, I'll show you as we go." They walked straight down the track entry. They stepped through a heavy plastic sheet that hung from boards in the roof. "Them's called fly pads, kid. They keep the air from escaping down the track." The face or solid coal was within a hundred feet of those heavy fly pads. "Easy, boy, that ain't bolted." With Homer's hand on his shoulder, he stopped. If Homer had not stopped him, he would have walked all the way to the solid coal. He could see there were plates with bolt heads sticking out in the roof. "Don't go past these bolts, kid. That roof could fall anytime. It don't take much to cripple you for life. You see these things in the roof, them's bolts. A machine drills a hole and then the bolt is stuck up in there. It has a shell on the end that is screwed on. When they put it on the machine, it spins expanding that shell. Them bolts suspend the roof forming a beam. That's how we keep it from falling in. But before that can be done, we have to put these jacks in place. Come on, I'll show ya." They each carried a jack and went to the edge of the bolt line. Homer took a bar and scaled down the loose rock. He took one of the jacks and placed it three feet from the last bolt on the left side. "These bolts are on three foot centers, boy. That is the bolt pattern. You set these jacks so you protect yourself. Don't ever go out from under the support of the bolts or the jacks."

They finished installing the jacks in those two entries. Then Homer showed him how to hang a curtain to direct the air. "We're exhausting the air off each entry. That means that we hang the curtain on the left side rib." Seeing Jesse's confused look he added, "Remember I said the return air is on the left side of the section." For the hundredth time, Jesse shook his head as if he understood.

Jesse's back was already hurting. Each one of those jacks weighed about twenty pounds. He figured that in a shift he would have to handle well over a hundred. His arms hurt from holding that curtain up and pounding in these triangular flat nails that Homer called spads. He began to wonder if this was such a good idea. He sure as hell did not want to be doing this the rest of his life. He continued following Homer around. They went into an entry that needed cleaned and dusted. Again, Homer showed Jesse how it was done. He had Jesse shovel the coal ribs and throw the coal out into the middle of the entry.

Jesse was working as fast as he could and he was winded. He looked at Homer who had not even worked up a sweat. Jesse thought, "He is at least forty years older than me. How the hell can he keep this up?" Homer never slowed down.

Just then a machine came into view. "That's a scoop, kid. That big bucket on the front is called a shovel. It will clean up the coal we shoveled. See how it articulates in the center. It can make real tight turns. It has a hydraulic ram in the center of the bucket that's hooked to a blade. It can shove everything out of the shovel." They picked up fifty pound bags of what Homer called rock dust. They threw this on the roof, ribs, bottom, and coal face.

Homer kept right on working and explaining, "We put this stuff on to keep the coal dust from exploding in case there's a gas ignition. It's heavier than the coal dust. If we don't do this, a gas ignition would lift up that there dust and cause an explosion. Now do you understand why everything is so white? Make sure you get them coal ribs good."

"Why do they call them that?"

"Hell, I don't know. They just do." It was at that moment that someone set off an explosion. To Jesse, it felt like the very air was pulsating. It was like being in a steel drum with someone using a sledgehammer on the side. He did not know whether to run or hide. He just dove to the mine floor covering his head. Homer was laughing so hard that he nearly fell over.

"Get the hell up, kid. It was only a shot."

Jesse got up and brushed himself off. "What the hell is a shot?"

"They was using sticks of powder to shoot down the coal. When we get done, we'll go see how they do it." They continued working. Jesse was getting less and less enthusiastic as the shift wore on. He began to feel that you have to be nuts to do this kind of work.

They finally stopped for lunch. Jesse followed Homer back to the dinner hole. He was still not sure where he was. It was like a revelation when all of a sudden they came upon the crosscut where their buckets were.

Two other men were having lunch at the same time. The entire crew did not eat together. In that way, they could continue to mine coal. Homer introduced Jesse to the two men by saying, "This is the new kid. Them is Carl and Pete." They were about the same age. Jesse guessed that they were in their thirties. They were dressed just like all the rest. Their faces were smeared with coal dust. This made their eyes and teeth seem like snow white. Jesse wondered if his face was that dirty. Both men were lean and just a little taller than he was.

Carl was the first to speak. "Well, kid, what do you think of it?"

"It's not quite what I expected."

"Hell, the first day that me and Pete started, a rock hit me on the hard hat when we was coming in. I ran all the way to the bottom 'fore they could catch me." Everyone laughed at that.

"Well, it's okay but I won't be here forever." Jesse still had visions of paying off that new car and maybe going to school. He had always hated school but somehow it was starting to look better.

Pete spoke up. "You won't?"

Jesse shot back. "Nope, I'm here just to get me a stake for a car."

Carl said, "It seems to me that we thought the same way. That was twelve years ago."

"Well, I'm going to be different." Jesse quipped.

Homer butted in, "Hell, kid, some little girl is gonna set your britches on fire and you'll be screwed like the rest of us."

"There ain't no way. I got plans." Again, everyone laughed at his naïveté.

Homer pulled out his pipe and lit up. Jesse was shocked. As if reading his mind, Homer said, "Boy, don't do as I do. Just do as I say." Jesse just sat there in silence until their lunch was over. He tried to sift through what he had heard. He knew that he would not be like these men. He had plans.

They got up to leave when they noticed someone making a circular motion with their cap lamp. Homer said, "Come on, boy, someone wants us. That there is how you signal people down here." They walked down the entry towards the main track. They finally got close enough to recognize Gower.

"Hey, Homer, take the kid and go into the main return. There's a man door just across from the section track switch. The midnight crew left some tools in there just inside the door. Bring them bars back to the bolters."

Homer started out without answering. Jesse just kept on following. They got to the airlock on the track and walked through. It surprised Jesse how much pressure was on those doors. Homer then led him across the track to a small door in a concrete block wall that Homer called a stopping. It was awkward getting through the door with all that they were wearing.

Homer grabbed Jesse's shoulder hard. "Watch where you're walking, kid. This is where the guys come to take a dump. Remember, you only take a crap in the returns."

Jesse thought that he was in an outhouse as soon as they stepped into the return. It sure smelled it. It smelled much like the outhouse back home. That smell was mingled with sulfur and decaying wood. He noticed moss hanging from the timbers in rolls. It reminded him of his mother's drapes in their living room. They seemed to be rolled and pleated. They found the tools. He took two of the rock bars and so did Homer. Jesse had one hell of a time getting back through the man door. He fell face first trying to get out. Homer just shook his head.

They walked past a place where several metal hooks hung on the trolley wire. They were all attached to cables. Homer told him, "These power all the machines on the section. They run by direct current. If anyone asks you to pull a nip for a certain machine, this is what they are talking about. You see those brass tags? Them are what tells you which machine."

Jesse had no idea how he would remember all this stuff. When they got back to the section, they went to the No. 2 entry. They were loading coal in that entry. Homer explained, "That there is a loading machine. It's on tracks with the controls on the right side. The front is called a shovel. It has what's called 'gathering arms' to scoop up the loose coal. They load the coal on them cars called buggies. They have a chain conveyor in the center. You see how that man is seated facing us. Well, when he goes to leave he turns around in the deck and kicks that seat up and he is facing out. You never turn them things around." Jesse just kept shaking his head as Homer talked. What he remembered was that machine was almost as wide as the entry. He wondered how you were supposed to walk around without getting hit.

They went into an entry where a cutting machine was being used. It had four rubber tires and the operator sat in a deck that was only four inches off the mine floor. A huge metal blade stuck out from its front with a chain on the outside of the blade. Homer explained, "This undercuts the coal. We do this so when we shoot the coal has someplace to go." Jesse could not believe the dust. He could hardly see Homer and he was right next to him. He wondered how men could work in this stuff. He began to appreciate the sacrifices that these men made.

Just as soon as that cutting machine left, another machine that Homer called a coal drill pulled into the entry. This was also a rubber-tired machine. This one had a long boom that had augers used to drill the coal face. "This machine drills the holes that we put the dynamite in. We put four across the top and three in the center." As this machine was moved, Jesse saw a light come around the block. He could not tell who it was. The man yelled, "Hey, Homer, get your ass out of there. I'm going to shoot." Homer quickly moved out with Jesse following close behind. They had no sooner moved when they heard the man yell, "Fire in the hole!" He did this three times and then the explosion came. Jesse knew that it was coming this time, but still he jumped.

"I got one more thing to show you, kid." Homer told him. They found themselves back in the entry where they had set the jacks. This time another machine was being used to put bolts in the roof. "You see that boom there? They stick an auger with a bit on it into that head. That is what's called a stab jack just below the head. That holds the machine steady and allows the hydraulic pressure to force the auger into the mine roof as it rotates. We are using three foot bolts. They drill the holes about forty inches. They then put a bolt on that head. They shove it all the way into the hole and then turn on the rotation. There is a shell on the end of the bolt that expands locking it into place. They have to follow the same pattern as we did putting up the jacks. You understand?" Again, Jesse shook his head. "This is the most dangerous job on the section. We get more men hurt and killed doing this than any other job in the mine. Gower will probably put you on this job tomorrow." Jesse began to get a sick feeling in the pit of his stomach. He could not honestly say if he would be back tomorrow. He again looked at that rock drill they call a bolter.

Jesse asked, "Why would they put someone like me on that machine? I don't know nothing."

"'Cause it's so damn dangerous and it pays a low rate. It's for the new men."

The rest of the shift was spent doing the same things over and over again. They kept shoveling, rock dusting, hanging curtains, and placing jacks. By the end of the shift, Jesse was numb. His back hurt, his throat was sore from the dust, and he was soaking wet from sweating. When it was time to go, Jesse climbed into the coal car with his coat and bucket in hand. He leaned his head back against the side of the car and immediately nodded off to sleep. It lasted about two minutes. Bang! Bang! Bang! There was a sudden jolt as the cars began to move.

Jesse was far less enthusiastic on the way out than he was on the way in. The price that he would have to pay for that new car was higher than he thought. He sat in silence for the ride to the bottom. He filed out with the rest and walked to the cage. He could not believe how stuffed they were on the cage ride up. Everyone was fighting to get out. The banging and crashing seemed louder this time. Then came the oppressive heat about forty feet from the top. The sunlight about blinded him. The men bolted from the cage to get their cigarettes, cigars, and pipes. He felt drained. He had no desire to run. In eight hours, his whole view of life had changed. Why would anyone want to do this kind of work? Why would any man risk his life for money? Why the hell was he here?

When they got to the top of the stairs at the bath house, Homer reminded him to put his light on charge and pull his tag. Jesse could not believe the guys were knocking him out of the way.

When he got into the bath house, he found most of the men were in the shower. The guys were screaming, laughing, and a lot of horseplay was happening. He saw one naked man chasing another, snapping a towel on the man's behind. His first thought was, and they call me "kid".

By the time he got into the shower, all the hot water was gone. He was sore, he was tired, and now he was freezing. This was not what he had in mind. He thought this was just his first day and already he hated it. There was no way that he would stay for a lifetime. He could not understand why anyone else did.

The parking lot was nearly deserted when he got to his car. The old clunker back fired as he tried to start it. He again thought of that new car that he was going to buy. Yeah, it was worth it he thought to himself. It will only be for a little while.

CHAPTER 20
IN AN INSTANT

Those that God loves do not live long.

—George Herbert, *Jacula Prudentum*

Jesse stared at Connie and their eight-month-old son. He could not believe how happy he was. He had a good job, the woman he wanted, and now a son. It had been four years since he got hired at the Y&O mine. He had become a coal miner with great reservation. He had gotten his car and he had gotten his girl. Circumstances dictate your life he thought. The need for money and stability kept him in his place.

"Hey, Connie! You coming to the game?" Jesse yelled.

Connie stepped to the door of the basement so she would not have to yell. "Sure but it will be a while. The baby is still sleeping."

"Well, I'm going, honey. See you there."

Jesse played on a UMWA league baseball team and today they were playing at the New Town baseball field. It was only a quarter of a mile from his brother's house so he walked. It was early June and it was such a beautiful day. The sun was shining and the birds were singing. It was a great day to be alive. His mind was still a little in the clouds as the second inning began, and still no Connie. He wondered what was taking her so long.

Connie had been caring for little Jesse and had not been watching the time. When she realized that the game was slipping away she rushed to get there. She loaded Jesse Jr. into a baby buggy lent to her by her sister-in-law and started towards the ball field. It was such a beautiful day that she began to hum her favorite song, "Can't Help Falling in Love." As she walked towards the highway a coal train was lumbering across the trestle and the clank-clank of the wheels crossing the track joints even added more music to her mood. As she got to the highway she noticed the copper waters of the creek which was on its long journey to the Ohio and down to the Mississippi she was overwhelmed with emotion. Her mind was somewhere between heaven and earth as she thought of her two Jesses and the love that filled her.

It was the fifth inning and still no Connie. Jesse began to worry. His daydream was interrupted by the crack of the bat and a ball whizzing towards him. He missed that ball but caught up to it and bailed it home. The jeers that he received made him cringe as he walked back to his position. Again he was distracted. This time it was a car that he noticed moving erratically as it came off a bridge about a hundred yards from the field. It was heading towards town and everyone could tell that the driver was either very drunk or falling asleep or both.

Connie had walked under the trestle and moved to the creek side of the road so she could face traffic. It was not a conscious thought that drove her there because her mind was still in the clouds. Those thoughts would be forever with her for she did not see that big black Packard that came flying around the turn. The driver would later tell the police with great slurring gasps that he did not hit anybody. Just a little bump that was all. That little bump was Connie and little Jess who would be together forever.

Jesse and everyone at the ball field had heard the crash. They all rushed to the trestle. At first all they could tell was that the car had nosed off the road into the creek. Then someone noticed the baby buggy wedged between the right fender and the tire. They found the baby whom they could not recognize. It was then they fanned out to search for who was pushing that buggy. The car had hit Connie so hard that she had been thrown ten yards to the opposite bank obscured by the heavy growth. Jesse's brother Tony found her there. She was already gone and he quickly looked for Jesse who was also searching. Jesse was only ten feet away and Tony could see the horror in his eyes. Tony tried to hold him back but it was useless. He would never forget that look in his brother's eyes.

CHAPTER 21
CLARITY AND SHAME

Nor ear can hear, nor tongue can tell, the tortures on that inward hell.

—Lord Byron

Buck Storm was about as miserable a human being as ever existed. Those who knew him were always glad when their business was concluded and he went his way. It had been almost twenty years since the war, but his memories were as fresh as if it were yesterday. Each night he relived that tragic day so many years before. He lived alone now. His mother had died many years ago. She had died in peace knowing that her intolerant and frightening son would exact her vengeance upon her faceless enemies. His loneliness would often drive him to seek companionship. He found it with whores in the large towns that were not too distant. When home, he wandered the rooms of that big mansion like a viper waiting to strike anything that came within reach. A bottle was never far from his hand during those hours when he fled from sleep. His nightmares were constant and all the alcohol did was make them more vivid. He often thought of Jamie and in his solitude would often cry out to her. But when he sobered up each morning he returned to his savage self.

He had hired a young woman from Cony to clean his house and prepare his meals. Her name was Nora. She was a rather plain and a very quiet lady.

She was twenty-eight years old and already contemplating a lonely life. She felt very sorry for Mr. Storm as she called him. Each time they were together her heart went out to the man. She never shared how she felt for she was a very proper young woman. She would remain at the house until supper dishes were cleared and return early each morning to prepare breakfast. This ritual was repeated each day for many months until one fateful evening. A storm was raging. The rain was pelting the house so hard that it rattled the windows. She could hear the wind howling so strongly that she decided to stay in the kitchen until the storm passed. She knew that Buck was in the house but he never bothered her. What was worse he ignored her completely.

It was twenty years ago on that night that Buck's nightmares began. He had drunk more heavily than ever before. But every time he closed his eyes he saw the lifeless faces of that boy and girl. He reached for the table to set his bottle down and missed. The bottle crashed to the floor shattering into a hundred pieces. Screaming with rage he staggered to his feet and went in search of another bottle.

Nora did not hear the door of the kitchen open. The storm was so violent that the thunder came in a steady roll like the volley of cannon. Buck had not seen her or she him until he bumped into a chair startling her. She cried out but then recognized him, "Mr. Storm!" He did not answer as he moved unsteadily towards her. When he was barely a foot away he stopped and stared for a long moment then he reached for her. He pulled her to him kissing her hard on the mouth. She did not resist. His passion became uncontrollable. He pushed her face down on the table hiking her skirt as he did so. In one stumbling movement he entered her. He pounded against her body with ever increasing fury. He came with a blinding scream of rage. Without a word he pulled from her and staggered from the room. Nora laid there sobbing for what seemed like hours. She had just lost her virginity to a man who had not showed her respect or tenderness. He had not even held her. No woman could manage forgiveness for such an act.

Storm was not drunk enough to forget what he had done that night. He kept trying to justify it. But for the first time in twenty years he again felt shame, for an unforgivable act of his own making. What he had done to the children was not intentional even though it consumed him. The woman was another matter. He had cruelly used her and he could not blame it entirely on the alcohol.

He had not expected her to come back to the house. The next morning he was staring out the window and saw her going to the side door at the kitchen. He left the house by another entrance and did not return until well past dark. He drank less that night as he tried to understand why she would have ever returned.

Nora continued to work day after day for nearly a month. Storm avoided her that entire time. Her only hint that he was still around was the money left on the kitchen table at the end of each week. Then it happened. She missed her period. She returned to the house and called out to him. Within a few moments they met in the hall. "Mr. Storm, I'm pregnant." He never said a word. He just turned and walked away. She returned to the kitchen and sat at the table sobbing.

Buck was clear headed this morning not having any alcohol since yesterday. He had returned to his room and thought about what must be done. He rationalized that he needed a cook and housekeeper. He also would have a place to go for sex without causing a scandal. At the end of an hour he sought her out. She was still in the kitchen weeping when he found her. "Marry me tomorrow," he ordered her.

Her response was a meek, "Yes, Mr. Storm."

The following morning he led her to his car and they traveled to Hagerstown, Maryland, where they were quietly married. Their drive had been in stone silence. Nora did not dare look in his direction. She stared out the window at the awaking land. Spring still was in full bloom. She hoped that it would wash this dull cloud from her mind. He was just the opposite. He now had purpose. He had reasoned correctly that without this purpose his self-pity would destroy him. He actually had a smile on his face, something not associated with Buck. He had made up his mind. Nora would be his legal concubine. She would raise his child whom he would bestow everything that life provided him. The child would be his purpose. This would redeem his soul.

CHAPTER 22
DISASTER AND REBIRTH

The bow is bent, the arrow flies, the winged shaft of fate.

—Ira Aldridge, *On William Tell*

70 TRAPPED AS THUNDERING EXPLOSIONS RIP COAL MINE

—*Wheeling News-Register*, November 20, 1968

Jesse sat staring at the television. Walter Cronkite was giving his analysis of the never-ending war in Vietnam. He then turned to the mine explosion at the Farmington No. 9 mine in Fairmont, West Virginia. The screen showed the huge plumes of smoke that vaulted from the mine. It had been nearly two days since the explosion and no word on the fate of the trapped men, which now numbered seventy-eight. Jesse's brother walked in as the segment began to air. "Any new information yet?" Tony asked.

"They're just starting." Jesse answered sloughing in a chair with his leg thrown over one arm.

The camera panned the scene with the heavy smoke pouring out of the mine shaft. Jesse was about to say something when he heard Tony Boyle's name mentioned. Boyle, the President of the United Mine Workers Union, was about to hold a press conference. He listened to Boyle give a passionate defense of Consol Coal Company, the owner of the mine. Tony and Jesse both sat in stunned silence. Jesse jumped from the chair. "How could that son-of-a-bitch get on TV and say such a thing? He hasn't a clue how or why that mine exploded."

Tony was livid. "I can't stand that bastard. I bet old John L. Lewis wishes that Boyle never was appointed president." John L. Lewis had been the long time head of the Union. He had retired in 1960 and had appointed a man by the name of Tom Kennedy president. Kennedy had died three years later. His death gave Boyle the coveted position. Boyle ruled the Union with an iron hand occasionally throwing a few crumbs to its members, to keep them satisfied, like getting them paid holidays and two weeks' paid vacation in the 1966 contract. But even the workers began to sense that their dues were nothing more than Boyle's own personal fun money.

"I wish someone with balls would come along and run against that asshole," Jesse fumed.

Tony just smiled at his brother. "Remember me telling you about Pa going to that convention in the 30's. He said that a guy got up to say something when John L. was talking and Lewis's men beat the shit out of him right on the convention floor. Then dragged him outside and dumped him right in the street. At that time 99% of the Union was behind Lewis. Now what do you think old Boyle would do if he thought that he was losing his grip on the Union? I think you need a beer, little brother. Maybe that will cool you off."

"Na, I'm going home. See ya later."

On the drive back to Adena, Jesse thought about his life. It had been nearly eight years since Connie and little Jess had died. He was nearly out of his mind for weeks. When he returned to his senses he had become somewhat of a recluse. He never hung out with the guys anymore. He worked and spent time with his brother and nephew. He lived with his mother and mostly kept to himself. When he felt the need he would visit the whorehouses in Wheeling, West Virginia, but he had chosen not to have a woman in his life. Now this, the Union that he loved was being corrupted by Boyle. His mom had raised him to believe that the Union and the government were his saviors. "By God," he swore, "If I can, I'll help bring that son-of-a-bitch down."

The next morning was like the first morning of his life. He had a purpose. He was going to help those men who worked in the mines. Yes, somehow he would help. Jesse never told anyone about what he planned, but he began to spend more time with the men and he started to voice his opinions. Everyone noticed the difference in him.

When he was finally able to return to work after the deaths in his family, the superintendent gave him the option of returning to the section at his old job or taking one as a fire boss. He asked for the fire boss job. Instead of being one of sixteen he would be alone. He wanted it that way. They put him on dayshift and there he stayed. He was one of the youngest men at the mine and that had not gone over well with the older men. But the company could put anyone in any position.

His day now began at 5:30 AM. He entered the bath house and found his basket, then sat on that very long bench, one of many. After putting on the heavy clothes and boots he grabbed his mine belt and hard hat. He then went next door to the lamp room and pulled his mine light from the charging rack. He removed the brass tag that hung below the lamp and placed it on a large board. His check number was stamped into the tag and it corresponded to a tag that was riveted to his mine belt. He also picked up his flame safety lamp that allowed him to check for methane and oxygen. He would spend a few minutes talking to the lamp man whose job was the most envied at the mine. He always smoked a last cigarette and stowed his lighter and cigarettes in a little shanty by the mine shaft. Then he would get onto the cage and signal the hoist operator by pushing up on a plunger activating a vacuum whistle. He rode the cage for the five hundred and fifty feet to the bottom of the shaft. He exited the cage entering an airlock, a cemented room about thirty feet long, with large metal doors on each end. Only one door could be opened at a time without disrupting the air. He would then find what he called a jeep for the ride into the mine.

The jeep was a small track mounted buggy that could hold four to six men. He unhooked the spring loaded pole which had been stowed. The pole which could be swung in both directions was placed on the trolley wire giving the buggy power. He moved the machine from the hole where it had been parked. He then moved through a switch. He stopped short of the main rail line and got on the mine telephone to contact the track dispatcher. The man cleared him for the forty-minute ride to the deepest section in the mine. When he arrived he had to throw a track switch that allowed him to enter the section track. He then had to open a ventilation door that prevented the air from escaping down the track. He parked the jeep in a crosscut that had track laid for that purpose. He then began his day.

His first duty was to pre-shift the mining section.

The intake, the fresh air entry, was on the right side of the section. He began there. He removed the anemometer that he had in a leather carrying case on his belt. This allowed him to determine the air velocity coming onto the section. He then started across the section checking the mining face of each of the seven entries. He checked the oxygen and methane in each entry and crosscuts that were not holed through. He then placed his initials, date, and time at each location. When he had finished he returned to the track entry and got on the mine telephone calling his report outside. With this done he began his walk for the day. He might walk the intake to the surface or maybe the return. The mine had been in operation for over forty years and it took several fire bosses to check the entire mine in the designated time intervals.

He wandered the mine like a ghost. He very seldom saw any of the other men during the day. He would be on the mine phone calling out his reports and wandering through the old workings making sure the air courses and the escape ways were free of obstructions. Some of the areas he traveled were mined years before his birth. He found old animal pens with the wood covered with the initials and dates of men who had passed that way long before him. He even found his father's initials in two locations.

With his decision to get involved, he was glad to have the fire boss job. It would allow him to roam freely throughout the mine and he would be able to observe and talk with most of the men. Being a fire boss, he carried the weight of responsibility for the lives of everyone entering that mine. It was he who had to make sure that no explosive gas mixture existed. It was he who had to make sure that areas were safe for the men to work in. It was he who had to determine if enough oxygen was present to support life. He reveled in the task.

As more days passed and it became apparent that the trapped men in Farmington No. 9 would never be recovered, the howls could be heard throughout the mining communities and then throughout the nation. Congress began to call for more stringent mine enforcement and a man came forward to challenge Boyle. His name was Jock Yablonski. Jesse thought, this is it.

CHAPTER 23
THE ADJUSTMENT

Coming events cast their shadows before.

—Thomas Campbell

*COAL MINE HEALTH AND SAFETY ACT TO
BE EXAMINED IN DEPTH IN MAY*

—*Cadiz News Herald*, April 2, 1970

Buck Storm was also listening to the news on that November morning. He was taking a sip of coffee when he heard of the disaster at Farmington No. 9. Being a fatalist he gave little thought of the consequences of that grim event. He went about his work as usual. He gave men hell and continued to be his miserable self.

It was not until spring of 1969 that he began to sense that something was about to change. That something would affect his way of life. The clamor from the explosion at Fairmont was being propelled by the turmoil in the United Mine Workers Union. Yablonski was challenging Boyle for the presidency of the United Mine Workers Union. The papers, television, and radio were constantly calling for more enforcement and stricter laws to protect the miners. Buck began to pay attention when Congress started to take a strong interest. Buck Storm began exploring other means of conducting business. It became apparent that a new mining law would be enacted by Congress. He had access to over five hundred acres of land where he controlled the mineral rights. Most of the acreage that Buck owned had been mined at the turn of the century. It contained Pittsburg No. 8 coal that the locals called Big Vein. He had approximately sixty acres of virgin coal. The remainder would have to be re-mined. He knew that the most cover over that coal was a hundred feet or less. He had made up his mind. He would surface mine that coal.

He would strip the earth from the coal. He would need a few machines such as dozers, loaders, and trucks. He knew that the new laws would be concentrated on the underground mines. Surface mines would be an afterthought. That should keep him away from those new regulations and the do-gooders they would be sending out.

CHAPTER 24
THIS IS MY UNION

Strong and bitter words indicate a weak cause.

—Victor Hugo

BOYLE LOSES DIST. 6 BUT DEFEATS YABLONSKI

—*Cadiz News Herald*, December 11, 1969

Jesse had decided to contact Yablonski and offer his services. He called Yablonski at his home and made arrangements to meet the following day. That night he could hardly sleep. His dreams were a mixture of him being a saint and sinner. At times he pictured himself as single handedly vanquishing Boyle, and the next instant ridden over by the forces of evil. He awoke early the next morning and put on his best clothes, a cotton shirt and jeans. He jumped into his 1956 Chevy Bel Air, his first and only car. That car was his pride and joy. It was black with a black and white vinyl interior and was spotless. Yablonski lived in California, Pennsylvania, which was in Washington County. It was only about sixty miles away. Whenever Jesse drove he was in heaven. It was his only pleasure since he lost his family. He had taken Route 250 to Wheeling and then traveled the new Interstate to Washington County Pennsylvania. He could not believe how much time that the new road saved. He hated this time of year. Everything was so brown and drab. He kept thinking of all that men like his father had died for. He knew that great struggles lie ahead and the fights they would have to endure. Men of conscience would always have to be vigilant and fight against men like Boyle.

He found Yablonski's home without too much trouble. When he knocked on the door, a man with craggy features and about his height greeted him.

"I'm Jesse Kamin, sir."

"Come in, it's cold out there." Jock replied.

Yablonski showed Jesse into his office and Jesse quickly came to the point of his visit. "Sir, I want to help you win this election."

"Well, I'm sure gonna need help. Boyle has already let it be known that this is his Union. How long you been in the Union?"

"A little over ten years. I'm a fire boss at the mine."

They talked for well over an hour. Jesse liked this man. He was blunt and inspiring. This was the type of man he could respect. He knew that Jock had been part of the problem that they would be fighting, but if he had the guts to stand up to those problems, Jesse had the guts to stand by him. They would keep in close contact over the next few months. Thus began the most intense time of Jesse's life.

He became Yablonski's spokesman in the United Mine Workers District 6, which covered all of eastern Ohio and northern West Virginia. The District had always been a hotbed of radical unionists. There were diehard supporters of Boyle, but they were outnumbered. Jesse found many supporters within his own local but was shocked at the animosity that some held for him. Even his own mother was against his support of Yablonski. She kept reminding him that it was Lewis that had ordained Boyle as president, and that was all the proof that she needed that Boyle was the right man for the job.

It was during this time that Jesse's closest ally deserted him. Tony Jr. had decided to join the Army. He had enlisted in July and Jesse was devastated. "Why do you wanna join the Army?" Jesse asked.

Tony looked straight at Jesse. "Ya know, Jess, this war is the biggest thing that is gonna happen to our generation and I don't want to miss it."

"You're nuts. This UMW election is the biggest thing that is going to happen to us." Jesse snarled.

"Hell, Jess, come December people will forget all about this shit."

Jesse just shook his head. "You're wrong, Tony."

"Well, I bet it won't be the last time." With a big grin he said, "Let's go get a beer."

The election was held on December 9. Boyle was elected in a landslide. Yablonski and his supporters were well aware that the election was stolen from him. He asked the Department of Labor to investigate the election. He filed several lawsuits against the Union. Jesse last visited Yablonski on December 15. He and several other supporters were discussing their next course of action. It was then that one of the men asked. "Did you see that white car? That's the third time that it has driven past here." The man turned to Yablonski, "You'd better watch your ass, Jock." That was the last time that any of them would see Yablonski alive.

Jesse had spent Christmas and New Years with his family. Tony Jr. was on leave and they spent every spare moment together. It was one of the best times that Jesse had experienced in years. The night before Tony was to return to his post they were watching TV when a news bulletin flashed on the screen. The commentator announced that the bodies of Jock Yablonski, his wife, and daughter had been discovered by his son at their Pennsylvania home. Jesse was stunned. He was always aware of the danger that Jock was in, but never once thought that his family was also in that same danger.

"I can't believe that anyone would kill his wife and daughter," Jesse stormed.

Tony Jr. turned to him and said, "I guess you got your own war, right here. You just watch your ass, Jess. I don't want to be getting a letter from Pop telling how you got your head blown off."

"Don't be worrying about me. You're the one they are going to be shooting at," Jesse snarled as he wrestled Tony to the floor.

Unknown to the boys, this would be the last time they would ever speak.

When Jesse had returned to work there was a lot of speculation as to who had committed the murders. The vast majority believed Tony Boyle was behind the murders. Jesse was not one of them. He just believed that Boyle was not that stupid.

He told them, "Boyle had access to professional hit men from the mob anytime he wanted them. They would not have murdered Jock's wife and daughter."

Within three days the guilty men were arrested. One was related to a low level United Mine Workers official in Kentucky and the others were drifters. As the conspiracy unfolded Boyle was finally indicted for the murders. Jesse was incensed at the arrogance of Boyle and his henchmen. This violent act would set in motion a decade of such turbulence that none in the coalfields could have anticipated.

CHAPTER 25
ANOTHER WAY

The integrity of men is to be measured by their conduct, not by their professions.

—*Junius*

UMWA OFFICIAL EXPECTS AT LEAST 3-WEEK STRIKE

—*Wheeling News-Register*, November 11, 1974

In the fall of 1974 the men in the coal mines went on strike. The date was November 12. The miner's contract with the coal companies had expired. During their forced vacation Jesse and his brother Tony Sr. decided to tear down a barn on their mother's property. They borrowed a tri-axle dump truck from a friend. This person also was going to allow them to dump the scrap wood from the barn on his property. It was being strip mined by a local company and the discarded wood could be buried. It took them several days to complete the project. On their final trip to the strip pit they stopped and talked to two mechanics who were working on an Allis Chalmers 41 bulldozer. This was the biggest dozer yet built for this type of work. It had one flaw. The final drives, the gearing that propelled the machine, were weak and quickly destroyed themselves and had to be replaced.

The company that employed the mechanics had

voluntarily shut down operations during the strike but continued the maintenance of their equipment. These men were friends of both Tony and Jesse. They lived in the little town of Harrisville, which was only three miles from their mother's farm.

"Hi, Tony. You guys are working harder than when you work," a big bear of a man exclaimed.

Climbing down from the truck Tony answered. "You know what it's like working for your mother. She's a slave driver." Jesse walked around the front of the truck laughing.

The mechanic who hailed Tony was about his age. They had gone to school together. His name was Steve. He was what Tony and Jesse's Union brothers would have called a scab. They were working for a non-Union outfit.

A fuel tanker was parked within a few feet of the dozer, which was jacked up on wooden crib blocks.

"Hey, Steve, you got that fuel tanker sitting pretty close to that dozer you're cutting on. Is it full?"

"You're damn right, it's full. Hell, you would have to light it on purpose to get that fuel oil burning." Steve answered.

The other man, a tall lanky fellow, asked, "You guys heard anything about the strike?"

Jesse offered, "We heard that a bunch of pickets took pot shots at a tipple over by New Philadelphia yesterday."

"Yeah, we heard that too," Steve replied.

The men talked for a few more minutes with Tony finally saying it was time to leave. As the brothers swung up into the truck Jesse yelled back. "You guys stay out of trouble. See you later."

While driving away neither brother saw the twenty

cars of Union pickets approaching the mechanics from the opposite direction. They drove home talking mostly about hunting. Rabbit season had just opened and they were both anxious to try out a new dog. When they arrived at the house Jesse heard the fire siren as soon as he opened the door. As both men looked towards Harrisville they saw a huge column of black smoke climbing into the air. Both knew at that moment what it was. They literally flew back to the pit that they had just left.

The fire department was already there. They both searched for their friends. They could not find either man. They asked the men from the fire department what had happened. The heat was so intense that the man in charge had everyone move back at least five hundred feet. The fear was that oil reservoirs would begin to explode on that dozer.

"It looks like someone opened them valves on that tanker then lit the oil. Ain't no way that we can put that out." At that moment there was a tremendous whoosh as one of the tanks on the dozer exploded. Flames were shooting two hundred feet in the air. The tanker never exploded but that fuel oil burned for hours. When it was done the dozer was a complete loss. It had gotten so hot that even the dozers blade was destroyed.

It was not until late that night that they finally found Steve hiding at his home.

"It wasn't two or three minutes after you guys left that they came. There were twenty car loads of them with five or six in each car. They told Slim and me to get the hell out of there and not to come back till this strike was over. Hell, guys, they said that if we went back to work or told who was there, they'd burn our houses down." Steve was still shaking as they tried to console him.

On their drive home Jesse told Tony what had been on his mind for a long time. "Tony, I have been a strong and outspoken Union man my whole life. What you told me about Pa and the way things were in the old days, we had no other choice, but it has changed since Yablonski died. It's as if idiots have taken control. There has been one wildcat strike after another with all kind of senseless violence. I've had enough. I was going to tell you and Mom together but after tonight, well, I want you to know that I have applied to the Mining Enforcement and Safety Administration. They are looking for experienced men to enforce those mining laws. Maybe I can do our people more good there. I've had it with the Union."

The 1974 strike ended with the richest contract in the United Mine Workers history. But the wildcat strikes continued and the violence increased. Both Jesse and Tony knew that something had to give. Tonnage at the mines had dropped so low that they were lucky to get five tons per man. In their father's hand loading days the men averaged ten tons a worker.

CHAPTER 26
BLACK GOLD

Our Lord commonly giveth Riches to such gross asses, to whom he affordeth nothing else that is good.

—Martin Luther, *Colloquies*

ENERGY SHORTAGE CREATES DARK DAYS FOR LABOR FORCE

—*Wheeling News-Register*, January 4, 1974

Buck Storm looked out over his land holdings with a great big smile. The OPEC oil embargo of the year before had driven up the price of Big Vein coal from a few dollars a ton to an astonishing $109.00 a ton. The new contract he had in his hands was going to make 1974 a very good year.

Storm was distracted by a dust cloud coming up the road onto his property. An old beat up car came into view. It had government plates. The car pulled right up to his truck. The driver a small wiry man of about forty said, "Are you Mr. Storm?"

"Who the hell are you?" Storm shouted.

"The name's Carter, Frank Carter, I work for the Mining Enforcement and Safety Administration."

"What the hell do you want?" Storm, growled.

The man already on edge answered. "I'm here to do an inspection."

"Get your ass off my property, and I mean now." Storm screamed.

Carter returned to his office without confronting Storm. A swift trip before a Federal Administrative law judge forced Storm to accept federal inspectors.

It was not one of Storm's better days. He could not intimidate or bullshit the judge and when the judge informed him that the inspections would take place with or without his cooperation, and under the control of Federal Marshal's, he then relented.

Thus began a fiery relationship between the government and Buck Storm.

CHAPTER 27
THE GREAT COAL STRIKE

For Satan finds some mischief still for idle hands to do.

—Isaac Watts, *Against Idleness*

WELFARE AND OTHER AID READIED FOR MINERS

—*Cadiz News Herald*, December 8, 1977

"Well, gentlemen, you didn't think we were going to let you set on your ass till this was over, did you?" The words came from Will Bailey, manager of the St. Clairsville, Ohio office of the Mine Safety and Health Administration. The organization's name had been changed with the signing of the new Federal Mine Safety & Health Act of 1977.

For the past two weeks, the men had been in the office receiving annual training required by the agency. A coal mine strike had started on December 6, and the agency decided to keep the men in the office until it was over.

"I got a paint brush for each one of you and the paint is in the hall. Now get busy."

The office, a large leased complex with at least twenty rooms, was a challenge. The thirty men began the job of painting ceilings and walls. The seventeen women office workers were busy with filing the massive amount of paperwork that the men produced.

Most of the men including Jesse Kamin were happy to have something to do. It made a long day just sitting around doing nothing.

Jesse and his friend Larry Jackson were busy painting the office that they shared with two others. It was a claustrophobic cubical with four metal desks, bare painted walls, fluorescent lights, and two file cabinets. "How do you think that this is going to end, Larry?" Larry wiped some paint from his face and just shrugged his shoulders.

"The way things are going, it's a terrible time to strike." Jesse lamented.

Larry stared at Jesse, "It's never a good time. You're worried about your brother, ain't ya?"

"Yeah, he isn't getting any younger. You save up for these things and every three or four years you get wiped out."

Larry said, "Hell, now they can get food stamps while they strike."

Jesse laughed sarcastically, "Only the ones that ain't got any pride. I've seen men that work seven days a week be the first ones in line to get them stamps. The ones that need them would die before they would go for them."

"Well, Jess, it ain't no sense worrying. It's about quitting time. Let's get the hell out of here."

The strike dragged on into January and the men completed painting the interior of the building. They did not even get a thank you from the owner, who did not have to pay one penny for labor. The men began to get restless again and make-work projects were not enough to keep them busy. Finally one project was to send men out to see if any of the strip mines were producing any coal. Jesse was one of the men sent to check them out. He was in a four-wheel drive just a few miles from St. Clairsville, Ohio, when he rounded a turn and had a blow out.

When he got off the road he found all four tires were flat. He had run into an area sabotaged by Union strikers. They had covered the road with what looked like rocks but were actually nails bent together to puncture tires and prevent coal trucks from hauling. A very pissed off Jesse had to walk close to a mile to get to a phone. This was happening everywhere. The longer this strike lasted, the uglier it would become.

Wildcats were a plague on the industry and since the death of Jock Yablonski in 1969 they had gotten worse. The unsanctioned strikes were started for any reason. Mostly they were started by men who did not want to work and they spread quickly shutting down every mine in the valley. All it took was one picket to stop a mine. The workers would not cross a picket line, even if it was a solitary man. If the companies could not stop this lawless behavior there would be no end to this strike. The Union district in eastern Ohio had become one of the most notorious for wildcat striking. The men would go out for any reason at any time. Working two or three days a week made it pretty hard to raise a family. No one could stand up to the hard cases, usually single men who did not care if they worked or not. Jesse's gut told him that it was going to be a long strike and who knew how it would end.

CHAPTER 28
LEGENDS GROW

The injury we do and the one we suffer are not weighed in the same scales.

—Aesop, *Fables*

Buck Storm was not a happy man. He had not moved any coal since December 6 and here it was February 2. He was sitting in his pickup watching his men work on the equipment. His mine was about a mile off the main road that ran into Barton, Maryland, right off Georges Creek. He had decided to go along with the local coal association and not antagonize the United Mine Workers by trying to produce coal while this strike was on. He gazed at the sculptured mountains covered with snow. It was his kingdom and he was really galled that someone could dictate to him what to do.

It was in the midst of this festering anger that he got a call on his radio. "Hey, Buck, you got a dozen car loads of pickets at your gate." Buck climbed out of the truck pulling a Remington 30-06 rifle out of the rack, behind his head. The men heard him say, "It's getting so a man can't breathe." He headed for a front end loader parked close by and got it moving down the haul road. His anger built as he went. The men gathered at the gate were in no mood to be messed with. They had been drinking for hours and had enough courage to do about anything. They heard the machine coming and could see the great clouds of dust spewing behind the giant loader. Storm stopped about fifteen yards from the gate and jack knifed the machine to block the road. He exited the cab rifle in hand.

One of the men in the crowd yelled, "Well, if it ain't the guy that owns the place."

Buck answered in a cold harsh voice. "Yeah, I own it and I'll shoot the first sons-a-bitch that comes through that gate." Some of the men laughed and one yelled out, "Let's call his bluff." They started forward, but the only problem was that Storm was not bluffing. He shot the man in the lead and chambered another round as the men began to scatter. In just a minute, there was only one vehicle, a pickup truck, near the gate. Buck got back in the loader and drove by the wounded man. Forcing the teeth of the bucket right into that new pickup truck, he lifted it off the ground and proceeded to destroy it. By the time his workers got to the scene Buck was standing over the injured man with his foot on the man's neck. One of his men yelled, "We better call an ambulance."

Buck said, "Fuck the ambulance. Call the sheriff."

After the police arrived and an ambulance finally called, Buck walked up to the sheriff. "Clager, tomorrow I'm going to be hauling coal. I'll have armed guards on every truck with orders to shoot to kill if any sons-a-bitch tries to stop them."

The sheriff incredulous said, "You can't do that."

"You just watch me."

The sheriff left and called the Governor's office with word of what had happened. After a harrowing night he finally got word that the state police would escort the trucks to prevent further bloodshed. As for the man whom Storm had shot and whose new truck had been destroyed, he was charged with trespassing. Storm did not even receive a reprimand. If anything, he became a folk hero on Georges Creek.

CHAPTER 29
A COAL MINER'S WIFE

What is sauce for the goose is sauce for the gander.

—Tom Brown, *New Maxims*

Another drama was unfolding not far from Georges Creek. This one was more private. A woman stood working in her kitchen preparing for the return of her husband, who was a Union miner, out of work, because of the strike. She was born in these mountains. The town was called Kempton. It was only a few miles from where she now lived. Kempton, West Virginia, located in Preston County was a barren treeless community at the time of her birth. Kempton was a typical coal mining camp with rows of clapboard houses, a tipple, a bath house, a company store, with not much for the children to do but play in the dirt.

Chris Nolan was in her late forties: lean, attractive, but hard as they come. She had been distracted all day. This strike was causing a lot of pain and there was no end in sight. She was tired of Jack, her husband, going off and boozing with his buddies all day while she was stuck working at home. She heard the pickup pull into the garage. He was home.

Jack, normally a jovial guy, was a terrible drunk. He was a tall man, lean and hard from working the mines since he was thirteen. He stepped into the kitchen not even bothering to say hi. Chris took one look at him. Disgusted, she said, "Drunk again." As mean as he ever was when drinking he struck her with his fist knocking her to her knees. He made a nearly fatal mistake. He turned his back on her as she came off the floor with an iron skillet in her hand. She swung the skillet just as he was turning to face her. He could not react quickly enough as iron made contact with bone. In most marriages this would have been a game changer, but within a week they were back living together as if nothing had happened.

CHAPTER 30
TRAGEDY STRIKES

Adversity introduces a man to himself.

—Anonymous

Jesse sat staring at the TV with little interest. Dallas had just scored another touchdown while Denver appeared weak. He guessed that 1978 was going to be a long year for Denver fans. He had been waiting weeks to see this Super Bowl game, but circumstances would not permit enjoyment. He stared at his brother Tony who was lost in thought. He had not been the same since the death of Tony Jr. who had gone off to Vietnam. He had volunteered as a door gunner on a helicopter. His helicopter was shot down on some unnamed hill on June 1, 1971. It was hard to believe that it had been nearly seven years, but to Tony it was like yesterday.

"Hey, Tony, you think Carter is serious about invoking Taft-Hartley?"

"Yeah, I think he is but I don't think it will do a damn bit of good." Tony answered without much enthusiasm.

"Yeah, I guess he's got his own problems and it won't help much pissing off the AFL-CIO."

Tony shifted in his chair. "I'm betting Miller won't be president of this Union for long. He's about a waste as a leader. We are going through all this bullshit and in the end we will come out with nothing. I heard a guy say that your generation screwed this up, but it was my generation that led yours. Whatever happens the glory days will be over."

The strike ended and as Tony predicted the men took a beating. He guessed that was the way that it would always be. He returned to work knowing that he would never be able to make up for all those lost wages. Work became drudgery for him. He hated going to work everyday. He could not concentrate. All he ever thought about was poor Tony Jr.

One day in late October he was asked to double over. He did not want to but they were hurting for men to operate a section. He stayed on the section between shifts and helped clean up and apply rock dust. That white powder always made him feel clean. The section foreman came through running the faces, checking for gas, air and hazards.

"Hey, Tony, how 'bout, jumping on that buggy for the remainder of the shift?"

"Whatever you need."

Tony never liked running this style of machine. It was called an off-standard buggy, because it placed him on the opposite side of the entry from the loader operator. He checked the buggy out and sat inside waiting for the crew to finish their snacks and get their assignments from the foreman. Unknown to Tony and the foreman another crew had taken a spare loading machine and run it up the return entry to clean up a small fall. They had brought the machine back onto the section moving from the No. 7 entry and parked it in No. 6 entry just past the fly pads, those big plastic sheets that were used to course the air through the section. The boom of that loading machine was within five feet of those fly pads and whoever had parked it had shut the lights off. It was right in the route that

Tony had to travel to get to the belt to dump the coal off his buggy.

Jesse had just gotten to sleep when the phone rang. It was his boss. "Jess, they had a fatal tonight over at Nelms 1. How 'bout doing the investigation for us? I don't have any of the particulars. They called the field office supervisor and reported it. One of Cadiz's inspectors will be there."

"I'm on my way." Jesse answered.

CHAPTER 31
A NEW POSITION

Thou art weighed in the balance, and art found wanting.

—Daniel. V. 27

It had been six months since that terrible night when Jesse showed up to investigate the death of his own brother. He had gotten apology after apology from his superiors but that did little to ease the pain. His boss had come to him yesterday with an offer.

Dale Morris was Jesse's supervisor and he was genuinely concerned about Jesse. He stepped into the hall and hailed him. "How about coming in for a minute? There is something I want to talk to you about. Close the door, will you?"

"What do you need, Dale?"

"Jess, we know that you have been having trouble since your brother died. We'd like to take the pressure off and offer you a new job."

"What job you have in mind?"

Dale got up out of his chair and walked around the desk to face Jesse. "We want to know if you would take a surface job. We have an opening with Gabe about to retire. I know that it's less money but it would be a hell of a lot easier and you wouldn't be reminded of your brother's accident every day that you work."

Without hesitation Jesse said, "I'll take it."

Dale was surprised. "You don't want to think about it for a while?"

"Nope, I've been waiting for something like this for a long time."

Dale said, "It's yours, we'll start on the paperwork today and you can move in with the rest of the surface men tomorrow."

CHAPTER 32
CHANGE OF COMMAND

There's none so blind as they that won't see.

—Jonathan Swift, *Polite Conversation*

VOTE 3-1 AGAINST UMW

—*Cadiz News Herald*, December 19, 1983

Ronald Reagan was now President of the United States. Jesse watched with wonder at the animosity his fellow inspectors showed towards the new president. He personally was glad to see Carter go. He believed that he was the most honest man to ever be president but he was no leader. His concern now was that things would move in the opposite direction and go too far. The Mine Safety and Health Administration policies favored the Union under Carter and now he guessed they would favor the companies.

Times were bad for the miners. Mine after mine was being closed. Between the EPA and the bad economy it could not get much worse. The headlines of the local papers were concentrating on the news that the UMWA was attempting to organize one of the local independent coal operators. Jesse would not have thought much of it except in this instance he would become directly involved. In 1977 the Coal Mine Safety and Health Act had been rewritten. A clause in the Act was now put to use by UMWA. It said that the miners could have a designated representative to protect their rights. A Union organizer had himself named as that representative. Of course, the coal company would not recognize this individual. So now the battle began. Almost daily complaints against the coal company began to flood the St. Clairsville office. Within two days, Jesse was given the assignment of answering each complaint. Every one required an investigation. A trip to the mine to see if the complaint had merit and then a written report would follow.

One of the phone messages stated that a dangerous condition existed at one of the strip pits. When Jesse got to the location he found that the pit had been completely reclaimed. This daily harassment continued right up until the scheduled vote.

Jesse was by himself as usual watching television when the program was interrupted with a special announcement. The Union's bid to organize the coal company had failed, dramatically. In fact when the votes were tallied less had voted for the Union than had signed the cards that initiate the process. After that night, the Mine Safety and Health Administration never received another complaint about that company.

In the late 70's the Mine Safety and Health Administration had hired a large number of inspectors and now the problems began. With so many mines closing the work force was out of balance at places like St. Clairsville. They had a great many inspectors and little work. The transfers began. At first they were voluntary, with most of the men choosing to go west. Then with Reagan's promise to reduce government the reduction in force or RIF notices began to arrive.

Harley Reynolds, Field Office Supervisor for the surface inspectors, called the men together. "It looks

like you two are going to get caught up in this layoff."
Addressing Jesse and a fellow surface inspector, "You
both have been with the agency for some time but you
know that is not how it works." Jesse knew how it
worked. The workers would be placed in three
categories: No. 1) Veterans with a Purple Heart, No. 2)
Veterans, No. 3) Non Veterans. You could have years
as a non veteran and be bumped by a vet with only a
few years. Jesse was in the latter category. His sour
attitude was not helping either. He just did not care.

Jesse had taken a few days off and was asked to call
the office each day to check on the RIF. He called on
his first day off, a Monday. "Hey, Sandy what's
happening?"

Sandy Owens, one of the clerk typists, was beside
herself. "Jess, you're not going to believe this. Harley
got transferred out west. The rest of you guys are safe."
Three men had been transferred to other offices and no
one had lost their job.

Instead of rifting where the problem existed the
government chose to allow it to be regionwide. So
Harley, a grade GS-12 with high time in seniority,
bumped out a new hire out west. The musical chairs
were fascinating to watch. In fact, some of those rifted
actually started higher paying jobs, with the
government. Within a few months every worker
transferred was returned to their original duty station.
Untold millions had been spent for nothing and great
hardship for those involved.

Jesse's attitude became worse by the day. This was
the best job that he ever had and he hated it. The
death of his brother plagued him and the ridiculous
things that were happening at work added to his
frustration. He became miserable to be around.

"Jess, what the hell is wrong with you? You can't pull this crap. You use to be the best inspector that I had." Harley said, with disgust. "It almost looks like revenge for your brother's death."

"You guys hired me to enforce the law. That's what I'm doing."

Harley shook his head. "Enforce it yes, but not use it as a whip."

Jesse became furious. "Tell you what Harley: let me know what you want and I'll do exactly as you say."

Disappointed, Harley said, "You used to be a gentleman. Now I don't know what you are."

Harley's problem was about to be solved. The coal companies had been complaining to the District Manager in Vincennes, Indiana, about Jesse's attitude. This is 1984, they cried, we do not need this kind of harassment. The manager was determined to correct the problem. In a meeting of District Managers he happened to express his problem to the manager of the Morgantown, West Virginia District, who was in dire need of an inspector in Oakland, Maryland. So after a few drinks and the presentation of a good bottle of Scotch the Jesse problem was solved.

Jesse had orders to go to the Mine Academy in Beckley, West Virginia. This was the Monday following his little discussion with Harley. He came into the office, checked his messages, talked to Harley for a few moments, and left. It took him about five hours to drive to Beckley. He liked the Academy but hated the drive. The last fifty miles on the West Virginia turnpike were a pain.

The Academy was like being on vacation. It had everything: a great gym, a full size indoor pool, sauna, Jacuzzi, racquetball, and a great cafeteria. In its beginning they had required two men per room but that had changed and now each man could have a private room. It had a modern design and there were steps everywhere. The guys joked that for a safety academy it was an accident looking for a place to happen. When Jesse entered the building he went straight to the registration desk in the residency area. A message was waiting for him to call back to his office. He dialed the number.

"It's Jess, let me speak to Harley."

It took Harley two full minutes to get on the line. "Jess, I got bad news. You've been transferred to Oakland, Maryland. They want you to report there next Monday."

"I just saw you a few hours ago. Why didn't you tell me then?"

"Jess, I just found out. That's the God's truth. I would have rather told you face to face."

"Hell, Harley, I'm supposed to stay here for two weeks. I can't possibly get there that soon."

"Call Morgantown and tell them. I'm sure they will accommodate you."

Frustrated, Jesse said, "OK, I'll see you when I get home."

He made the call to Morgantown and it was agreed that he would report to Oakland on October 1. That gave him one week at home before he had to leave.

PART II:
A NEW BEGINNING

CHAPTER 33
OAKLAND FANTASY

Every man's life is a fairy-tale written by God's finger.

—Hans Christian Andersen

It did not take Jesse long to get his affairs in order. He had a small apartment in St. Clairsville that he had lived in for the past four years. He did not have a lease so it was easy to leave at the end of the month. There was no woman in his life other than his mother. She had remarried several years ago and was happy with a man that Jesse respected. His other siblings were scattered throughout the Midwest and he only saw them occasionally. With Tony and Tony Jr. both dead he did not have much in his life at all.

He felt quite alone on that drive to Oakland. It was a sunny day when he crossed Cheat Lake on Route 48 and started into the mountains. Just as he rounded the first turn for that great climb they began to play the theme from Star Wars on the radio. The majestic mountains, the rousing music, and the excitement of the unknown all played on his emotions. He was no kid anymore. He was nearly forty-four years old and about to start a new life. It was a bit disconcerting. He thought of what he would be doing. He knew that these mines had been inspected for many years. He decided that if he found problems that the companies were not told about he would allow them to fix the condition without writing a violation. If they refused he would then force them. He felt it was the only way to be fair.

One of his friends who knew the area told him to take Route 42 at Friendsville, Maryland, to cut off a few miles of his drive. This would take him to Deep Creek Lake. The lake was only ten miles from Oakland. When he intersected Route 219 he began the last few miles of his journey. He crossed a large narrow steel bridge putting the lake on his left. He was surprised that very few businesses existed along the lake's boundary. There were some newer homes but many more small cottages. He had to admit that he liked the scenery and the quietness of the place. He saw a couple of bars and some restaurants. There was not much here.

When he arrived in Oakland he stopped at a big fruit market to ask for directions. He knew that the MSHA office was located in the post office. He found that he was only a half a mile from his destination.

Jesse had just pulled up in front of the post office when he saw one of the prettiest blondes he had ever seen. She was talking to another attractive lady and disappeared inside the building. There was something about that woman that really made an impression on him.

He saw the MSHA sign on the side of the building and walked in that direction. He started down a stairwell of ten steps and walked into the office. He was in a hallway that had two office doors on his right and the hall extended into a large open bay with four desks. He walked into the bay and found the office clerk filing some papers.

"Hi, I'm Jesse Kamin."

"Well, it's about time. We thought you got lost," said the hard looking women. "My name is Chris, Chris Nolan. I think the boss will want to see you pronto."

An office door opened. A tall heavyset man stepped out. He appeared to be in his late fifties and was dressed in jeans and a flannel shirt. Jesse did not think that he had shaved or combed his hair in a day or two. "The name's Paul Barnes. I'm the field office supervisor." Jesse thought his words were just a little bit slurred. Jesse stepped up and shook hands with the man. "Step into my office and we'll get started."

Jesse turned to the woman. "Nice meeting you."

The room like the rest of the office was like a dungeon. It had bare walls, no window, with a single file cabinet and a desk. Barnes started, "Did they tell you that you'd be on per diem for the next ninety days?"

"Yeah, they did." Jesse replied.

"Did you find a room before you came in?" Barnes asked as he pulled open one of the desk drawers. He had two glasses and a bottle of Jim Beam in his hands. "How 'bout a drink?"

Jesse was beginning to get a little on edge as he answered. "No, thanks, I still have some driving to do. I have to go out and find a place to stay."

Just then Barnes noticed two of his inspectors talking to Chris Nolan.

"Hey, Frank, Mick, come in here." He yelled. "Guys, I want you to meet Jess Kamin." Gesturing to the men he said, "Jesse Kamin, this is Frank Carter and Mick Able." The men shook hands and Barnes said, "Frank, I want you to take Kamin out tomorrow and show him his mines. It will take you a couple of days so take your time." He then turned to Jesse, "You had better go find that room."

As Jesse stepped out of Barnes's office he walked over to Chris Nolan. "Mrs. Nolan, do you know of a good place to stay around here?"

"Mrs., my ass! The name is Chris and don't be forgetting it."

"Sorry, Chris, just trying to be polite." Jesse answered with embarrassment.

"I'm a widow, and I don't take crap from nobody. Now to answer your question there's a good little motel and restaurant. It's on the edge of town towards the lake. It's called the Starlite. They are reasonable and the food ain't bad either." Chris returned to her typing without giving Jesse a second glance.

Jesse just shook his head and walked out. When he reached the sidewalk he saw the same beautiful blonde exiting the post office. He watched her until she entered her car and drove away.

The Starlite was everything that Chris said it was. He explained to the owner that he would need a room for ninety days. He was told this would not be a problem.

He unpacked what little that he had brought and decided to take a drive and see what Oakland had to offer. He got on 219 and headed south. In a little over a mile he made a sharp left just past the courthouse. He came to a stoplight with 219 turning right and heading out of town. He decided to go straight. He drove up a grade and saw a Heck's Department store and a few other businesses. Among them was a movie theater. They were playing "The Evil That Men Do". Well that would take care of tonight.

CHAPTER 34
GEORGES CREEK

A stranger's eyes see clearest.

—Charles Reade, *The Cloister and the Hearth*

He met Frank Carter at 6:00 AM the next day. Carter was already at work filling out some papers. "Well, Kamin, at least you're on time."

"Did you think I wouldn't be?"

"Ah, forget it." Carter answered with disgust.

"No, what's the problem?"

Carter stared at him for a moment. "It's just that every time they send someone up here they think it's play time."

"Well, I don't know about everybody else but I'm here to work." Jesse barked.

"Just relax." Carter said apologetically.

Carter motioned for Jesse to take a seat. "There are four other guys working here that you haven't met. They won't be in till later. We might catch them this evening. If not, I'll make sure that you meet them tomorrow. Five of us are underground inspectors and the one guy is a training specialist. Wait till you meet him."

"What's that supposed to mean?"

With a grin Carter answered, "Nothing. Just wait and see. You're gonna love it here."

Carter grabbed his briefcase and said, "Let's go."

When they got to the street Carter asked, "Where are you parked?"

"Over there by the bank."

"Well, Jess, you're going to have to move it. You can't leave it on the street. You'll get towed. We all park down by the tracks. It's a public parking lot. Our government cars are parked there too. Go ahead and move it and I'll pick you up."

They were just passing the movie theater when Jesse asked, "Where we headin'?"

"We're on our way to Georges Creek. The majority of your mines are located there."

"How many ID numbers do I have?"

Carter glanced at him with a smile. "You got one hundred of 'em."

Jesse was stunned. "I only had twelve in St. Clairsville."

Carter laughed, "Well here you're gonna have to work. Anyway I heard Paul say that they were giving twelve IDs to our Elkins office. The rest are yours."

"Do I have any Union mines?" Jesse asked.

"Yeah, you have two. One is a United Mine Workers mine and the other is an independent. Most of these mines are small, two to five men. About twenty of those IDs are for tipples and plants. 99 percent of your operations are either in Garrett or Allegany Counties."

Jesse thought that at least he would not have to worry about the two Union mines. He smiled, "Ya know, until I started with the government, I didn't know that there was coal mining in Maryland."

"Don't tell anybody. We want to keep it a secret." Carter laughed.

"Do I have any bastards to deal with?"

"Yeah, only one. His name is Storm, Buck Storm. He's a born asshole."

"How have you guys been handling him?"

"I've been inspecting him since he chased off the last surface inspector we had. I did his first inspection and we had to take him to court just to get on his property. He really is a son-of-a-bitch. You're going to have to be careful around that one. He doesn't have any sense."

Jesse was more interested in the scenery than talking and he sat back enjoying the ride. They were on top of a large mountain that stretched for miles. He saw farms, private homes, and not much more. Then they started down what Carter called Backbone Mountain. Just as they broke the crest Jesse smelled a most putrid odor. He asked, "What the hell is that smell?"

Carter laughed again, "That is the Westvaco paper mill. Don't worry. You'll get use to it."

Jesse received another shock as they descended the mountain. He noticed places for trucks to pull over. There were large signs stating that it was mandatory for the truckers to stop. They had passed two such stops when he asked. "What are those for?"

"You will understand when we get to the bottom of the mountain." Carter answered. They passed several more of the stops and finally came to the bottom. It leveled out and crossed a bridge. Immediately the road made a ninety-degree turn. There was a large cement wall facing them as they crossed the bridge. It had several crosses painted on it. "All those crosses represent a trucker who died here. Before they put in all those stops many trucks would lose their brakes when they became so hot they wouldn't work."

"Just before you get on the bridge there used to be a gas station. The old fellow that owned it told me he was standing at the pump when the last runaway occurred. He said as the truck flew by the driver smiled and waved at him. He guessed that he was doin' at least seventy when he passed." They drove by the mill and through Luke, Maryland. Westernport was the next town. There they turned up Georges Creek. The contrast from the pristine mountain to Georges Creek was startling. Carter pointed out coal tipple after tipple and he saw draglines on the hillsides as they proceeded up the creek.

"How many draglines are there?" Jesse wondered out loud.

"We must have about forty-five. They're mostly Lima 2400's, Manitowoc 4600's and 4500's.

"I'm going to have to get use to all these small machines."

Carter laughed, "Small, you think they're small?"

"Hey, Frank, where I come from that's small. Your machines have a bucket capacity of 10 to 15 cubic yards. I was inspecting shovels that could move one hundred cubic yards of dirt on a single pass and we had one dragline with two hundred and twenty yard capacity. Yeah, to me they're small." Carter pulled off onto a dirt road near Barton, Maryland, to show Jesse some more mines.

"Oh shit! You're going to meet the devil sooner than expected." Carter mumbled, as a pickup truck pulled up beside them. "Hi, Buck. I want you to meet Jess Kamin, our new strip inspector."

"Jesus Christ, another pinko communist son-a-bitch, fucking with me. That's all I need." Storm shouted as he gunned the truck throwing gravel in all directions.

"Well, Frank, you were right. He's a born asshole." Jesse said with a half smile. But Frank noticed that his eyes weren't smiling.

They never stopped at any of the operations that day.

Frank kept pointing out jobs and telling Jesse more of the history of the place. Jesse had to admit that he liked what he saw. As they entered Frostburg, Maryland, Jesse noticed several references to Consol. There was even a street by that name.

Carter saw the questioning look on Jesse's face. "Bet you didn't know that Consol Coal Company started here in Frostburg?"

"No, I didn't."

"Yeah, way back in the 1800's. They mined the Big Vein coal. It's Pittsburg 8 seam. Here's another shocker for you. The first coal mined in this country was done right here on Georges Creek. Remember that town Westernport we drove through?" Jesse shook his head indicating he did. "Well, it got its name because they would take the coal in barges from there east when the river was flooded. That's how they got the coal to the eastern cities. They would then tear the barges apart and sell the wood. Pretty cool, huh?"

They stopped off at a McDonalds for lunch and Jesse kept eyeing everything. The terrain was different but he did like it. They returned to Oakland a different way. They were on Route 48 heading for Grantsville, Maryland. As they exited the four lane road Carter pointed to a large field with a historical marker at the edge of the road. "That's were Braddock's army camped before they went to Pittsburgh to get massacred during the French and Indian War. Hell, there's all kind of history up here. I'm going to take you the back way into Deep Creek Lake. We have several jobs up there." Carter stopped at one job that appeared to be abandoned.

"Doesn't look like much is happening here." Jesse volunteered.

Carter said, "Some of these guys only mine when they're in the mood. I knew that no one would be here. I wanted to show you the coal and I didn't want to get into anything today."

They got out of the Jeep and walked over to the pit. What Jesse saw really surprised him. The uncovered coal was laying on such a steep pitch that he wondered how a front end loader could work to extract it. "Man, I've never seen anything like this."

Carter laughed, "Well, they work pretty carefully and you'd be surprised how few accidents that we have. By the way, that same slope you see is at several of our underground mines, about seven of the fourteen we inspect."

Carter pointed out several more mines. Finally they came to the lake. Carter crossed over an old narrow steel bridge and turned up Route 219 to Oakland. He pulled to a stop in front of the post office and Jesse noticed the same beautiful woman that he had seen twice before. "Hey, Frank, you know who that girl is?"

"Nope. Never saw her before. The rest of the guys should be in. I'll introduce you."

Jesse watched the woman until she was out of sight. He could not figure out why he even cared but he did.

Carter yelled, "Hey, Chris, what's new?"

Chris laughed, "You're in early, that's what's new."

Jesse dropped his things on the desk and turned to face a giant of a man. He held out his hand. "Hi, I'm Jesse Kamin."

The giant with a huge grin answered. "Hi, the name is Craig Porter. Nice to meet you." Two other men gathered around them, both extending their hands. Porter made the introductions. "This here is Arney

Smith and Ed Cameron." Jesse shook hands with both men.

Jesse heard Frank yell out, "Hey, Chris, where is Booker?"

"He's in with the boss." She answered.

Frank headed right to the boss's office and within a couple of minutes returned leading a portly black man with a huge gray mustache. "Jess Kamin, this here is Booker T. Katts, our Training Specialist and resident preacher.

Booker reached out and shook Jesse's hand answering Carter with an "amen".

Jesse smiled and took an instant liking to this unusual character. He appeared to be close to retirement.

Paul Barnes broke up the bull session. "Give the guy a break. You'll have plenty of time to talk later. Frank, I've changed my mind. I'm sending Booker with Kamin for the next two weeks. I've got another project for you. Besides Booker needs to get out to the strips anyway."

Jesse asked Booker, "What time do you want to meet?"

Booker thought for a minute and said, "How 'bout 6:00 AM?"

CHAPTER 35
WORKING WOMEN

A woman is more influenced by what she divines than by what she is told.

—Ninon De L'Enclos

Jesse returned to his desk. He had to wipe off a layer of white dust. Not thinking much of it, he began filling out his time card for the week. The others were busy at their desks and Jesse really did not have time to talk to any of them. They began drifting out of the office in pairs. It was not long before he was alone. Chris had given him a key to the office so he would be able to come and go as he pleased. He picked a mine off the list for him and Booker to visit the next day. He did not have a clue where it was but he figured Booker would know. He decided to call it a day so he locked up and bounded up the steps making a quick left at the top. He immediately bumped into someone, knocking mail all over the sidewalk. "Why don't you watch where the hell you're going?" A woman shouted.

"I'm sorry." Jesse said as he picked up the mail he turned and glanced into the face of the beautiful blonde. She took the mail from his hands and headed into the post office without even a glance at him. He then noticed Chris Nolan standing by a car with the hood up. "Hey, Chris, what's wrong?"

"I can't get it started." She answered.

Jesse walked over and checked out the problem. He removed the air cleaner and had her try to start the machine. Soon as she hit the starter he saw the problem. He took a pencil from his pocket and lifted the flap on the choke and told her to try again. This time it started.

"What was wrong?" Chris asked.

"The choke was stuck. Come here and I'll show you what I did in case this happens again." While they were talking he noticed the blonde exit the post office. "Hey, Chris, do you know that blond headed woman just leaving the building?"

"Sure, her name is Beth Stewart. Why?"

Jesse gave the woman a long stare and answered. "Just curious."

"Jess, I want to thank you. That was a great help. I would have been stuck here for who knows how long."

"Anytime, Chris," he said, as he continued walking towards the parking lot and wondering about that woman, Beth Stewart.

CHAPTER 36
PREACHERS AND PROPHETS

The best prophet of the future is the past.

—John Sherman, Speech, 1890

Jesse arrived at the office at 6:00 AM sharp to find that everyone but the boss had beaten him.

As soon as he entered Chris yelled out, "Where have you been, sleepy head?"

"I thought you all started at 6." Jesse countered.

"We do," Carter answered. "But we come in early to talk and have a cup of coffee."

"Well, you ready, Kamin?" Booker shouted. "We got us a long drive. We'll use your Dodge Ram Charger. My car don't do well in them pits."

Kamin started the car and said, "I picked Raines Strip for today. It was next on the list to be done. You know where it is?"

"Yeah, I've been there a couple of times. It's just outside of Coney." Seeing the puzzled look on Kamin's face he added. "That's what they call Lonaconing, Maryland. They drove out Route 135 the same way as he had gone with Carter. Booker pointed to a restaurant and said, "How 'bout stopping there?"

This was something that Jesse very seldom did. He stopped for lunch on occasion but the only times that he stopped for breakfast was when he had meetings to attend. He always tried to get to the mines as early as possible.

When they entered the restaurant, the woman at the

bar called Booker by his name, "You're late. You want the usual?" Booker nodded. "And how 'bout you, big guy?" She turned to Kamin.

"Coffee will be fine," Kamin answered. He turned to Booker, "What did she mean by you're late?"

"'Cause I come here all the time." Booker smiled.

Just then Jesse became aware that everyone in the crowed place was staring at them and none too friendly. "I thought this was a friendly place. Why all the animosity?"

Booker took a while to answer him. He stared around the room and finally said, "Two reasons: one, they don't know you, and two, you're sitting with a black man."

"What the hell does that have to do with anything?" Jesse asked.

"Believe it or not, Kamin, there's still prejudice in this world." Booker smiled. "Counting me there's only one black man in Garrett County."

The waitress brought their order. "Anything else, fellows?"

"I'll have a piece of pumpkin pie as long as you are serving it, honey." Booker answered, with a big smile on his face.

"I thought you were a preacher?" Jesse asked.

"I am." Booker answered with a huge grin.

"Well, what the hell is this flirting?" A confused Jesse asked.

Booker stared at him for a long minute then answered. "God put all things of beauty on this Earth for us to enjoy and that's one of them. Do you ever read the Bible?"

Jesse scoffed, "I did once but no more. You see I found that no matter what, you get the shaft."

Booker looked at him and shook his head. "You didn't get the answer you wanted so you quit?"

Jesse took a sip of his coffee and said, "Let's skip it."

Booker knew better than to press someone who was in confusion about faith. He finished his breakfast in silence.

When they were on the road again Booker held his Bible occasionally reading a passage, stopping when he had to give Jesse directions. It took forty minutes to get to the mine site from the diner.

They pulled into the pit and the first thing Jesse noticed was how orderly everything was. That was always a good sign. He pulled up to a trailer that he took for the office. A man came out the door wearing a hard hat. It was the only thing that indicated that he was at a mine. "Mr. Katts, I didn't expect to see you so soon," the man said, as they exited the car.

"Mr. Bolton, this is Jesse Kamin, our new strip inspector." Booker said.

Jesse interjected, "I am here to do an inspection of your mine."

"Be my guest." Bolton said, "Just watch yourself in that pit. It's a little ragged."

Jesse perked up immediately. "We'll take a look at that first." As the three men walked over to the edge of the pit Jesse noticed fissures a few yards back from the edge of the highwall. Some of the fissures were two feet wide. When he got to a position where he could see the face of the face, he saw that it was undercut. There was a front end loader operating in the pit and a farm tractor with a brush attached to sweep the coal. Jesse turned to Bolton. "I want you to shut down and get those two men out of there." Bolton started to protest but Jesse cut him off. "I'm issuing an imminent danger order. No one goes into that pit until that overhang is brought down."

Bolton said, "I'll have to get hold of the owner. He will want to hear about this."

"Call whoever you want but no one goes into the pit." Jesse answered.

Jesse started to check the equipment while the foreman was contacting the owner. There were three trucks and two bulldozers working, besides the machines that he saw in the pit. He found all the machines in good repair and did not notice anything out of the ordinary. "This outfit seems to do it right." He told Booker. It was then that he noticed Booker seemed agitated. "What's wrong?" He asked.

"It's going to take hours for that owner to come from Baltimore." Booker said, "I've met him before."

"We'll wait for him. That's the least we can do." Jesse answered.

What Jesse did not know was that Booker had been verbally assaulted by this man and he did not want a repeat of it.

It took nearly four hours for Dalton Raines to get to the mine. In that time Jesse had completed the inspection and found nothing other than the highwall problem. When the owner did appear Jesse was surprised. The man was dressed in a business suit and overcoat. He was at least six feet, five inches tall with his head shaved. The man walked up to him with a large smile on his face and introduced himself. Then he started. "What seems to be the problem here?"

"I had to issue an order on that pit. The highwall is in danger of collapse." Jesse said.

"And who the hell are you, a geologist?" Raines seethed.

"No."

"Then are you an engineer?"

"No, I'm a god damn mine inspector and that pit stays closed."

With his attempt at intimidation failed Raines answered, "Well, eh, what can we do to fix the problem?" Jesse showed him what needed to be done and walked back over to where Booker and the foreman were standing. The foreman volunteered. "There's a fella up here named Buck Storm. If you pull this same shit on him they'll find you in ditch somewhere."

"Oh, I'll be careful. Don't you worry." Jesse answered.

"Just trying to be helpful." Bolton said.

"Call our office when you got that pit fixed and I'll come back and lift the order. Until then no one goes into the pit." Jesse said as he entered his Ram Charger.

"Booker, did you get the impression that Bolton would just love for me to get busted by that there Storm?"

"I know he would." Booker responded.

"Guess where we are going tomorrow, Book? I think I need to meet this Buck Storm." Booker cringed as they rode in near silence on their return to the office.

CHAPTER 37
WAR CLOUDS

Better pointed bullets than pointed speeches.

—Otto Von Bismark, Speech, 1850

The following morning Jesse picked up his car at the lot by the tracks. He noticed clothes piled on one of the government cars and more clothes lying beside it. It looked as though someone had thrown them there.

When he entered the office Chris greeted him. He had to tell her about the clothes. "You won't believe what I just saw," laughed Jesse. "There were clothes strung all over the parking lot and piled high on that green Jeep."

"Sounds like Arney's old lady threw him out again." Carter said, laughing as he walked up to the two.

"Never a dull moment here." Chris interjected. Booker came through the door, slamming it with a loud bang.

Jesse yelled over to him. "Are you ready to get going?" Booker's only response was a shake of his head.

When they got into the car Jesse noticed that Booker was being awfully quiet.

"You want to stop for breakfast?" Jesse asked. Booker shook his head no.

Finally Jesse said, "What's the matter?"

Booker finally said, "It's this guy Storm. He ain't got no sense. Years ago I was a Union organizer and we tried to organize Georges Creek. Well, one night some guys beat me near to death. While I was in the

173

hospital I found out it was Storm who hired them men. Another thing I found out was that the law up here won't go against him. You just be careful that's all."

"Booker, I was born careful." Jesse smiled.

When they arrived at the mine Booker again reminded Jesse to be careful. They both saw Storm's pickup at the same time. It was parked by a large front end loader where a mechanic was working. Jesse pulled in behind him. Walking up to Storm's truck, Jesse extended his hand saying, "Mr. Storm, I'm Jesse Kamin, the new strip inspector."

Storm just stared at Kamin with hate-filled eyes not even bothering to take Jesse's hand. "You're just another pinko communist sons-a-bitch coming here to fuck over an honest man. I don't like you and anything you stand for."

Jesse's temper began to flare immediately. "Listen, Storm, I got a job to do and I'm going to do it. Do I inspect or leave, your choice."

Storm thought for a moment before answering. He was deciding whether it was worth it to go to court again. He had lost the last time and was threatened with jail if he messed with inspectors. "Bart, come here. This son-a-bitch says he's an inspector. Stay with him and then come see me." Storm then put the truck in gear spinning out leaving the men standing alongside the road.

Jesse stared at the truck as clouds of dust rolled up behind it. He turned to the man Storm had addressed. "The name is Kamin and this is Mr. Katts. We are here to do an inspection."

"My name is Bart Kolb. I'm the mechanic and I take care of the pit."

"The first thing I want to check is the log book and then we'll check the pit." Jesse said.

The man produced the log and Jesse noticed his signature on the pages. "Are you certified to do the inspections?" Booker spoke up. "Maryland doesn't have a safety department so MSHA certifies the men to do the inspections. About all it amounts to is they want it and we give it to them." Jesse had not ever experienced that before. He glanced back through several weeks of inspections, and each page gave the date and that the conditions were good, and then they were signed by Kolb.

They were standing about seventy-five yards from the pit so Jesse decided to start with the mechanic's truck that Kolb was using. He was surprised when he found everything on the truck in good repair. Kolb volunteered, "The truck and everything on it are mine."

"He doesn't supply you with anything?" Jesse quizzed.

"Yeah, the oxygen and acetylene tanks, but that's it," answered Kolb.

As he got closer to the pit he realized that he was in a heavy equipment graveyard. There were frames of dozers and loaders lying everywhere. It appeared to him that they were cannibalizing the machines he saw scattered around. Jesse could usually tell if a problem existed with a machine just by watching it being operated. A 560 Hough front end loader was loading trucks out of a stockpile of coal and each time he reversed direction Jesse noticed that he was catching the machine in gear instead of using the brakes. He got the man's attention and had him shut down. "Hi, I'm Jesse Kamin, a Federal Mine Inspector. I would like to check your machine." The man started to get out of the cab. "No, just stay right there."

Jesse began by saying, "Just shut her down for a moment." He then walked around the machine. He stepped in between the left wheel and the frame. He saw a big problem really quick. There were no brake shoes on that wheel. He went to the other side and found the same thing. He called for Kolb to come over. "This machine has no brake shoes on either front wheel. I want you to park it until repairs are made."

"I'll have to let Storm know" was his only response.

The loader operator climbed down and asked Jesse. "What did you say your name was?"

"Jess Kamin." The men shook hands.

"Hey, Booker," Jesse yelled. Booker strolled over.

"What ya need?" Booker asked.

Jesse said, "How about checking the training records for these guys, while I check the equipment. Kolb will help you with that. He seems OK."

Booker went right to work and Jesse continued his inspection. It only took him about twenty minutes to shut down every machine that Storm had. It was for a variety of reasons, brakes, steering, machines missing rollover structures, you name it and Jesse found it. He was amazed that these conditions could exist in 1984. Surely they had been inspecting the mine since 1972. He walked over to the mechanics truck to talk to Kolb.

Kolb immediately asked, "Why the hell is everything parked?"

Jesse said, "That's what I came over to talk to you about." He began to explain to Kolb the problems he found when Booker interrupted him.

"Those ain't the only problems they got. They ain't got no records on any of the guys' training."

Jesse turned to Kolb, "When did these men have refresher training last?"

Kolb just shrugged his shoulders. "We ain't ever had any training that I know of."

Jesse just shook his head in disbelief. "You'd better get Storm over here."

It took less than five minutes for Storm to get to the pit. He came roaring in with dust and rock flying everywhere. The truck had barely stopped when he threw open the door running straight to Kamin. "What the fuck is going on here?" He screamed. "Why ain't them machines working?"

"I shut them down for a variety of reasons." Jesse interjected.

"Boy, you and me are going to be having words," Storm yelled.

Jesse stared at him for a long second before answering. "I will give you time to repair the equipment, but I am writing an order closing the mine until you get annual refresher training for these men. Call our office when you find someone to teach it. We will want to sit in on the training and monitor the class. One more thing. They get paid for all the time they miss."

Storm gave him a stare that made Jesse shiver in response. "You're a big feelin' son-of-a-bitch, ain't ya, boy. Well, you better enjoy it while you can."

"Are you threatening me?" Jesse quizzed.

Storm bit hard on his stogie and motioned to Kolb. They stepped away from the federal men, "Do what they tell you. I'll take care of that sons-a-bitch in my own way." He walked over to his truck and yelled to Jesse, "You deal with Kolb from now on. I don't even want to see your fuckin' face." With that he jumped back in his truck and sped away throwing stones everywhere.

It took Jesse nearly two hours to write all the citations and orders for the conditions that he had found. When he was finished he walked over to Kolb. He explained everything he had done and asked if he had any questions.

Kolb said, "Just a word of warning. The boss can be a real son-of-a-bitch. You had better be careful. You're the first person ever to set foot on this job and try to tell him what to do. It ain't going to end pretty."

"Thanks for the warning, but he won't mess with the Federal Government."

Jesse and Booker left the mine heading back to Oakland. They did not say much on the way. Both were deep in thought: Booker thinking that he might have to monitor Storm's training class and Jesse trying to understand how this guy could have gotten away with these problems for so long.

CHAPTER 38
AUTUMN GLORY

One crowded hour of glorious life is worth an age without a name.

—Sir Walter Scott, *Old Mortality*

17TH ANNUAL AUTUMN GLORY

—*Oakland Republican*, October 11, 1984

The office was deserted when they arrived. Booker was on his way home within five minutes. Jesse sat at his desk completing the day's paperwork. When he finally went back to the hotel he chose to go straight to the bar. He had a couple of beers and was about to leave when Ed Cameron, a fellow inspector, came in.

He pulled up a chair beside Jesse. "Well, Kamin, how is Booker treating you?"

Jesse laughed, "Booker is a character."

"You got that right. Did you notice that he keeps a Bible on his desk? But don't let that bother you cause he's a good sport. Hell, you can say almost anything to him and he'll have a quick comeback."

Jesse answered, "I've noticed already that he ain't a typical preacher."

Ed asked, "Where were you two today?"

"We were on Georges Creek. It was an interesting day."

"I never get up that way. I'm stuck underground every day." Ed moaned.

179

Finishing his beer, Ed said, "See you in the morning." Jesse waved and ordered another beer. He was disgusted with being in Oakland, the mess at Storm's, and for the first time he began to feel lonely and that was something for a man who had spent most of his adult life alone.

Jesse made it to the office at 5:30 the next morning. Chris Nolan was already at work. He said, "Good morning, Chris," as he poured himself a cup of coffee.

Her response was, "What are you doing in here so early?"

"I got a lot of work to do today. Why?"

Chris said, "Didn't anyone tell you?"

"Tell me what?"

"Those men," Chris said. "None of them are coming in today including Booker. It's because of the Festival."

"What festival?" Jesse queried.

"Boy, you must be blind. Didn't you see all them banners advertising the Autumn Glory Festival?"

"I haven't been paying much attention." Jesse answered.

"Well, Mr. Kamin, I think it's just what you need. There will be a lot of activities including a big dance on Saturday night. Every time I see you I get the impression that you are just like a lost pup. You need to get out and meet people. Start making some new friends."

"I hope that I have already made a couple." He answered.

"You're going to need a little bit more than this old lady and a crazy old black man." They both laughed.

He sat down in a chair in front of her desk and began to talk. It was surprising to him how open he was with her. He began with how he was forced to come to

Oakland with the story about being traded for a fifth of Scotch. Before he could really wallow in self pity Chris blurted out. "You got a woman?"

"No!" He had answered a little louder than he had wanted. Why did I shout that out, he wondered?

Chris stared at him for a moment and said. "That's your problem."

"You're wrong, Chris. That would just create a problem. I like my life just the way it is."

"Haven't you ever had a girlfriend?" She chided.

"I was married once."

"She threw you out is that it?" Chris laughed.

"She died."

"Oh, I'm sorry, Jesse." A flustered Chris answered.

"It happened a long time ago." At that moment the phone rang. Chris answered. "It's for you. A guy named Kolb." Jesse took the phone from her. After a couple of grunts of understanding Jesse hung up.

"The Company that Booker and I were at yesterday set their training up for Saturday. I'm going to go out and monitor their class. I want to make sure it's done right."

"Barnes will never pay you for an extra shift for Saturday." Chris said.

Getting up Jesse said, "I will just leave now and finish out my week on Saturday. I don't trust these people."

"You're going to miss out on all the fun. At least go to the dance. Promise you will at least try." She badgered.

"OK, OK, I'll try," He laughed.

Jesse returned to his hotel room. He was not looking forward to another night of nothingness. His sleep was interrupted by dream after dream. He saw himself in a mortal battle with this guy Storm and the next instant he saw the face of that beautiful blonde. He swung from bliss to fear throughout that long night.

The following morning he began a very long day. He drove to Lonaconing, Maryland, and found the garage where the training was taking place. He met the trainer, a fellow by the name of Rangle. His credentials were correct and Jesse let them proceed. Just before they began Buck Storm came into the room. He wore the same clothes that Jesse had last seen him in. He also had his ever-present stogie hanging from his grizzled face. The man stared at Jesse for the entire time that the class was held. If looks could kill it would be Storm's that could do it.

Jesse remembered his brother advising him when a bully was plaguing him at school. "It don't matter how afraid you are on the inside, just act mean as hell. He won't know the difference." So Jesse's stares were just as ice cold as Storm's with neither man blinking. When it ended Jesse felt as if a great weight had been lifted from him. He handed the papers terminating the order to Storm who just balled them up in his hands. Jesse turned and walked out.

Storm motioned to Kolb, "Your brother still works as a bouncer in Cumberland?"

"Yeah, why?"

Storm grinned, "Tell him to come see me tomorrow."

Jesse was tired by the time he returned to Oakland. He finished the office work as quickly as he could and returned to his room. There he debated about going to the dance that night. The more he argued with himself against going the more he dreaded being alone.

It was nine by the time he arrived at the dance. It had started at eight. He walked up to the bar and ordered a beer just as someone slapped him on the back. It was Arney Smith. "Well, Kamin, you getting settled in?"

"Yeah, doing just great," answered Jesse sarcastically.

Smith flung his arm in a large arc saying, "Take your pick. Any one of them would be more than happy to help you get over your, whatever it is you have. If you don't get it, half of them are either unhappily married or unhappily divorced."

As Smith talked Jesse spotted that beautiful blonde he had seen. She was seated at a table with five other women. "Hey, Arney, do you know anything about that blonde sitting over there?" He motioned towards the table where she sat.

"You aim high, don't you, boy? Her name is Beth Stewart. She's divorced with a couple of kids. Her old man was a lawyer that got his hand caught in the till. It was a big scandal. She's about the hottest piece in this here county and she's way out of your league."

Jesse never answered him. He just got up and started walking towards her table. She was just lighting a cigarette when he said, "Would you like to dance?" Startled she began to choke from the smoke. He gently slapped her back until she recovered.

"Yes, I would love to," she said, giving him a smile that could even melt old Storm, he thought.

"My name is Jesse, Jesse Kamin."

"I'm Elizabeth Stewart. My friends call me Beth."

"Does this mean we are going to be friends?"

She stared at him harshly and asked. "Who are you with?"

He hesitated for a moment and answered. "Absolutely no one."

She smiled as the slow dance came to an end. The

country band jumped into a faster paced song. Without missing a beat they continued swirling around the dance floor. As the second song ended she stared up at him saying, "That was fun, but I had better get back to my friends and by the way you are a very good dancer."

"Thanks for the compliment. Maybe we could do it again sometime."

She again gave him that great big smile answering, "I would like that." She turned and walked away with Jesse watching her every move.

He returned to the bar and found Smith grinning like he was privy to some secret that no one else could guess. "You had better tread lightly with that one. Her ex is about as mean as they come and he hasn't warmed up to the idea that she left him. Get what I mean?"

"It was just a dance." He answered, turning to take another look at her. To his disappointment, she and her friends got up to leave. He turned and finished his beer and without another word he left the dance feeling just as lonely as ever.

CHAPTER 39
THE BREATHER

The cold neutrality of an impartial judge

—Edmund Burke

On Monday morning Jesse arrived to find everyone had already gone including Booker. Chris Nolan was at her desk typing away.

"Hey, Chris, where is everyone?"

"They had to go to Morgantown for a meeting. They left about half an hour ago. Paul said to give you directions to one of the local mines so you wouldn't get lost."

"That was nice of him." Jesse answered as he flopped down on a seat in front of Chris's desk. "I want to thank you for telling me about that dance. It was sure better than being stuck in that room."

"Did you meet anyone interesting?"

"Yeah, Arney Smith was there."

"I meant girls, you bum." She laughed at him.

"Yeah, you remember that girl I asked you about, Beth Stewart. She and I danced a couple of dances."

"Is that it? Hell, I figured you'd be shacked up with someone by now?"

Startled, a flustered Jesse just smiled.

"You know, Kamin, you're the first forty-four year old I ever saw blush."

Laughing he answered, "You're the first woman I ever met that didn't give a damn what she said or to whom she says it." He got out of his chair and returned to his desk.

"Hey Chris, what is the name of that United Mine Workers mine that I have?"

"It's called Celex Mining. Why?"

Walking back to her desk he answered. "I need a breather after dealing with that Storm. How far of a drive is it?"

Chris lit a cigarette exhaling a cloud of smoke making Jesse cough. "It's only about a half hour away. My husband used to work there. One of my brothers still does. But I don't know how much of a breather that will give you."

"Let's just say that dealing with them will be less personal than these small family owned mines. Now how do I get there?"

She drew him a map as he pulled the mine's records for review. When he got to his desk he noticed white dust covering everything. "Hey, Chris, what is this dust over everything?" He yelled.

"Didn't anyone tell you about our asbestos problem?" She walked back to his desk and pointed to the pipes overhead. "Them pipes are insulated with asbestos and it's deteriorating."

"If this was a coal company we would be shutting it down. What the hell are they doing about it?" An angry Jesse asked.

"They sent some guy from the health group to take samples. We haven't heard back yet."

"How long ago was that?" Jesse quizzed.

"Oh, about six months."

"Jesus!" Jesse said as he waved her smoke from his face. "I guess it's inevitable. Either your smoke or the asbestos, one or the other will nail us."

"You're funny" was her only response as he walked out of the office.

Armed with her directions and the information he needed for the mine, he drove past the courthouse and turned right as she directed and headed off towards Kingwood, West Virginia. He passed through Crellin, Maryland, before entering into West Virginia; he spotted a sign that said Alpine Lake Resort. He made a mental note to check it out when he had time. The country was fascinating to him. The mountains were beautiful and the fall colors were still on display. He could imagine himself living here forever. The only thing that bothered him was the poverty. As he drove through the town of Terra Alta, he saw many buildings sitting empty. It was sad and it made him think of his hometown. It was just a hollow reminder of its former self.

He started down a huge mountain heading towards Kingwood. It was the county seat of Preston County. He wondered why these people lived here. What do they do for a living? As he crossed the Cheat River and entered into town, he also wondered why they built a city out here in the middle of nowhere. The streets were steep. He kept climbing to the top of the mountain. Then he started down. He had driven just a few miles outside of the city when he spied the entrance to the Celex Mining Company. Chris had told him that the mine was a little over a mile off the main road.

He turned in, traveling through a large steel gate. He stopped for a moment at the sign giving the company and mine names. It also had their federal ID number and West Virginia mining permit numbers. He noticed a rail spur to his right with a ditch forty feet across. It lay between the road and the track. He saw what he suspected was a cloud of coal dust in the distance.

He sat for a moment watching. He then started to drive. Within fifty yards, the road made a long turn to the right. As he came out of the turn he abruptly stopped. He could see for nearly a quarter of a mile and what he saw between the road and the track was unbelievable. He counted at least twelve rail coal cars lying in the ditch. Some were on their side and some were face down in that ditch. He saw a score of trucks, the wheels that the cars ride on, lying beside the track and in the ditch.

He began to drive. As he got closer to the mine he saw more overturned cars. He had never seen a sight like this. As he rounded the last curve he stopped again. The preparation plant was now visible. He saw three silos with one shooting plumes of smoke into the air.

What he had taken for dust was smoke. It was another sight new to him. He had seen silo fires and investigated one that had exploded. He had never found a company continuing to operate while the fire raged. Why was no one attempting to put out the flames? He pulled up to what he thought was the office. Then it began. A man was standing by the door as Jesse approached.

"Where's the boss?" Jesse asked angrily.

"He's inside, mister." The puzzled worker said.

Jesse saw a man sitting at a desk in the first office he came to. "You the foreman?" He again came off angry.

"Yeah, the name's Homer Gleason. Who the hell are you?"

"The name's Kamin. I'm a Federal Mine Inspector and I'm issuing you an order for the silo that's on fire. I want it shut down immediately."

"Hell, I can't do that. I have to let the mine know."

"Call them and have them clear their belts now."

"Mister, you don't know what you're asking."

"Call whoever is in charge and let me talk to them 'cause it appears that you aren't."

Gleason began to get angry as he grabbed the telephone and called the underground mine. It was three hundred yards further down the hollow. "There's some asshole here from the government that says he's shutting us down." He paused, "I'll tell him." He turned to Jesse pointing towards the mine. "He says for you to come up and talk to him. His name is Austin."

Jesse never answered. He went back to the car and drove up to the mine. Two men were standing at the door waiting for him. One was Will Austin, the mine superintendent. The second was Jared Davis, the safety director. As Jesse walked up to them there were no introductions, just shouting. The same protests that he had heard from Storm.

"Have you begun to clear your belts yet?" They continued to yell. He finally said, "I need to use your phone."

"What the hell for?" Austin quipped.

"I need to contact Morgantown and let them know you're refusing to comply with an order."

"Now we didn't say no such thing. We just want you to explain why the hell you're doing this." Austin replied.

Jesse shook his head. "You're running coal into a silo that is on fire for Christ sake."

"Hell, that silo is always on fire." Jared Davis added.

"Are you shutting down or not?" Jesse demanded.

Austin turned to Davis, "Tell them to start dumping on the ground and clear the belts." Davis began to protest.

Austin cut him off. "I know that we only have room to stock a day's production. This asshole will have to explain to the corporate boys why he put two hundred and fifty men out of work."

Jesse's response was, "Do one of you wanta go with me while I inspect that plant?"

"You go with him, Davis, and report back to me," said Austin.

"We will," answered Jesse before Davis could respond.

"Mr. Davis, who is the Union representative?"

"Jake Wyatt. He is also the president of the local. He will be at the train load out."

They waited at the main office for Wyatt to arrive. Jesse stayed outside while Davis made calls to inform the plant personnel that they were shutting down. From where he stood all appeared normal other than the silo fire. He noticed an old fleet side pickup truck coming up the road. The bed was so rotted that the sides were flapping like wings. It pulled up in front of the building. An older man stepped out. He was wearing bib coveralls and a heavy hooded sweatshirt. He appeared to be in his early sixties. "You the federal man?" He asked.

"Yes, my name is Jesse Kamin."

"I'm Jake Wyatt."

Jesse shook his hand. "I'm starting a regular inspection today. When I saw the silo on fire the first thing I did was issue an order closing it down."

"Hell, Mister, that silo is always on fire."

Jesse shook his head. "I really don't care about that. The company is going to put out the fire and keep it out. As soon as Davis gets back out here we are going to start. Do you want to go with us?"

"You're damn right I do." Wyatt answered with an edge to his voice. As they were talking Davis walked out of the office and joined them.

"We might as well go through the plant building first."

They each drove their own vehicle back to the plant office. Davis let the plant foreman know that he and Wyatt would accompany the inspector. He also told him that the plant would be down till further notice.

Jesse finally said, "Let's get started." As they walked to the entrance of the plant, Jesse noticed that coal was spilled everywhere. It was out in the open and did not present a problem. When he opened the door to enter the plant Jesse got another shock. It was so dark that he could barely see. When his eyes adjusted to the dark he could make out the steps to the next level. He also saw two overhead belts with coal spillage so deep that they were dragging coal. Those belts were twelve feet off the ground floor. He spoke, "I swore that I wouldn't write any unwarrantable failure violations on this first inspection but that is what you are going to get." *Unwarrantable violations* were the violation of law that the company knowingly allowed to exist. He never used this power lightly. The fines were large and the consequences severe.

Davis immediately began to protest but Jesse cut him off again. Jesse asked. "Is this normal for you guys?"

Wyatt spoke up. "We're running this plant with a skeleton crew. We clean the place up every weekend."

Davis added. "That coal isn't hurting anything down here."

Jesse started to get angry. "Not hurting anything! It's blocking your walkways and I'm guessing you got an elevator back there somewhere that you can't get to. It's also a fire hazard. I'll give you four hours to get this cleaned up." Davis went back outside to let Gleason know of the violation.

Turning to Wyatt, Jesse asked, "What the hell is going on here? Doesn't your safety committee make regular runs?"

Wyatt almost apologetically answered. "We make them but they keep telling us they'll shut the mine down if we make waves."

The plant was eleven stories tall and Jesse only made three that first day. He had so much to write that he did not know where to begin. He started with the order for the burning silo. He next wrote the unwarrantable citation, followed by twelve more citations. It was well after dark when he finished. He then held a conference with Davis and Wyatt. He explained to them that if he found another unwarrantable violation that was serious, an order would be issued. He explained that the order on the fires in the silo gave control of the operation to the Mine Safety and Health Administration. The company would have to submit a plan for safely fighting the fire. After much ranting and raving by Davis, Jesse finally called it a day.

Jesse drove back to Oakland in silence. He did not even feel like listening to the radio. He thought of Unions, particularly the United Mine Workers and the American Federation of Government Employees of which he was a member. The men at the mine he just left had all the power in the world. They could have prevented these dangerous conditions from existing. They had allowed themselves to be intimidated.

He then thought of his own circumstances. He was transferred against his will from one personnel region to another without a RIF. This was against the government's own rules. Yet when he complained to none other than the president of the National Council of Field Labor Locals, he was told that the government could do anything it wanted to him. He then thought of the asbestos problem that he and his fellow workers faced. Nothing was being done. It seemed that the government was a dog that never bit its own tail, but it tore the pant leg off any that crossed it.

CHAPTER 40
THE WEST VIRGINIA FEAST

The feast of reason and the flow of soul.

—Alexander Pope, *Book of Horace*

When he arrived at his office he stacked everything on his desk and left. He started back towards his room. He changed his mind and decided to stop at a local bar and get a drink. The bars around here were a little bit different from those he had known in Adena. For one, most were newer and catered to a different class of people. Most of the patrons were tourists or businessmen. He picked out one that appeared empty. He did not feel like company. He entered and found two men sitting at the bar. He walked past them and sat at the far end alone. He did not see anyone behind the bar so he just sat there and waited. He was deep in thought when a beautiful voice asked.

"Well, Mr. Kamin, how are you today?"

Startled, he looked up into the prettiest eyes he had ever seen. He started to stutter; finally he was able to say, "Hi, Ms. Stewart."

"Honey, you look as though you were just given another opportunity to improve your sense of humor."

He started to laugh. "I've been getting a lot of that lately."

She smiled. "What can I get you?"

"How about a Bud?"

"You want a bottle or draft?"

"A draft would be fine."

She walked over and grabbed a glass. "What brings you to this dreary place tonight?"

"I didn't feel like eating at the restaurant where I'm staying. Just trying something new."

She leaned over the bar and said. "Can I make a suggestion?"

"Sure."

"Why don't you try our specialty? It's called the West Virginia Feast."

"What the hell is that?" He laughed.

"It's a chili dog with a generous helping of coleslaw poured on top."

"Can I get fries with that?"

"Fries and a sandwich coming right up."

All of a sudden he felt like he was on the top of the world. He could not believe his luck. He was surprised that just being around her could lift his spirits so much.

While he was waiting for his order, the two men who were sitting at the bar got up and left. He kept watching for a glimpse of her as she fluttered around in the kitchen. She finally returned with his dinner. Acting like an eighteen year old, he sat tongue tied. He ate while she was busy cleaning glasses. As he finished he finally said, "Ms. Stewart."

She turned and walked towards him. "Yes."

"I heard there is a dance this Saturday at the Legion. Would you like to go with me?"

She smiled at him. "Sure, I think that would be fun, but one thing, I think you have to stop calling me Ms. Stewart. My name is Beth."

"That's great, Beth. Where do I pick you up?"

"I live at 109 F St. Mt. Lake Park. It's only a couple of miles from here."

"How about if I pick you up at 7:30?"

"It's a date," she said with a smile.

He handed her a twenty and said with a big grin, "I'll see you then."

CHAPTER 41
DANCE OF THE BUREAUCRATS

Society in every state is a blessing, but government, even in the best state, is but a necessary evil; in its worst state an intolerable one.

—Thomas Paine, *"On the Origin and Design of Government," Common Sense*, 1777

When he got to the office the next morning he found Paul Barnes waiting for him and Chris Nolan sitting there with a most worried expression.

Barnes got up from his chair motioning Jesse to follow him. They entered Barnes's office. Barnes slammed the door as Jesse entered and he began to scream. "What the hell did you do yesterday?"

"I started a regular inspection at Celex Mining."

Barnes became even more irritated. "Never, I repeat, never write an order like you did yesterday without coming to me first. You got that?"

Jesse was getting angrier by the minute. "I don't need your permission to write anything. If you don't like what I did, vacate it."

Barnes was not about to do that. He sat down in his chair and looked up at Kamin. "They called Senator Byrd's office and he personally called me. What the hell do you think you're doing?"

Jesse still angry answered. "I was doing what I get paid for. They weren't. Less than six months ago I had to do an investigation of a silo explosion. No one was killed but three guys were injured. Is that what you would rather have?"

"I want you to do your job without making waves. You got that?" Barnes screamed.

Jesse stared long and hard at Barnes and then got up without answering. He walked past Chris with a look that scared the hell out of her.

Barnes yelled, "I'm not through yet," but Jesse kept right on walking. Picking up his gear he went straight out the door, which he slammed so hard that it was a wonder that the glass did not shatter.

CHAPTER 42
THE CONSPIRATORS

And would'st thou evil for good repay?

—Homer, *The Odyssey*

Another meeting was taking place on that morning. It concerned Jesse Kamin. In the parlor of Buck Storm's home, three men sat conspiring to rid themselves of another bureaucrat who was too full of himself. They were Buck Storm, Bart Kolb, and Ralph Kolb. Storm spoke first.

"Ralph, we got us a problem that you can help us with." Ralph, the younger brother of Bart Kolb, listened attentively. Storm continued, "We got us this here federal man who ain't got the brains he was born with. He comes in here telling me what to do believing that he can do anything he wants without worry. I want you to cause him worry."

"What you got in mind, Mr. Storm?" A grinning Ralph asked.

"I want you to cause him a little pain. You think you can handle that, Ralph?" Storm answered.

Ralph, all six feet two inches and two hundred fifty pounds of him, stirred from the chair. "Just let me know when and where. I guarantee you that son-of-a-bitch will have a lot to worry about. I got me a buddy who loves to do things like this for fun. I'll just ask him to come along. He will get a kick out of it."

Storm smiled, "I just happen to know where that bastard is going to be this Saturday night."

Just then the phone rang. Storm barked a greeting and immediately smiled. Covering the receiver, Storm said, "Excuse me, it's my boy."

CHAPTER 43
FRIENDS AND ENEMIES

Foul whisperings are abroad.

—William Shakespeare, *Macbeth*, Act V. Sc. 1

Jesse arrived at the Preparation Plant still fuming over his discussion with Barnes. He pulled into the parking lot near the mine office. He found Jared Davis, Safety Director, and Jake Wyatt, Union President, waiting for him. Jesse put his coveralls and rubber boots on saying, "Let's walk the belts today. Then we will get into the plant." They walked about fifty yards and climbed onto the first belt. They were standing at the belt drive. Jesse shook his head and asked, "Where the hell is the guard for this roller?"

Davis was the first to respond. "That pipe is the guard." The pipe he was referring to was a frame welded around the drive roller.

Jesse's words were like a hammer to Davis. "I'm issuing you a citation for the guarding. Guards have to be built in such a way that no one can reach past the guard and make contact with the pinch point. The only reason that I'm not issuing you an order is because our people have been accepting this for years." He had not even moved ten feet when Jesse asked, "Where the hell is the emergency stop cord on this beltline?"

"We don't have one." Davis answered.

"We ain't ever had one." Wyatt volunteered.

Jesse continued the inspection and found over fourteen thousand feet of beltline without emergency stop cords. All the beltlines drive rollers, take up rollers, and tail rollers were all guarded with pipe. Jesse could not believe what he was finding and it was 1984 for God's sake. The day continued to go downhill. At every turn he found more violations. At the end of two days he had written a total of thirty-six citations and orders.

It was his second long day in a row. When he finally returned to the office he found a note from Barnes telling him not to leave the office until they talked. He just dumped his things on his desk and left.

He traveled to his motel and went straight to the bar. After his third beer he saw a good-looking brunette walk in and she walked straight to the bar and sat down right beside him. "Hi, my name is Midge Rollins," She said.

"Jesse Kamin." He answered.

She was a beauty. "Have we met somewhere before?" He asked.

"You don't remember me. I'm crushed."

"I'm sure I would have remember you if we met. Where was it?" Jess added.

"I was sitting with my girlfriend Beth Stewart when you asked her to dance." She faked a pouting pose and laughed.

"Would you like a beer? Let me make up for ignoring you on that night?"

"Sure, I'd love it."

He had to admit, who could have missed such a looker. She had long black hair and she filled out her jeans as if she had been sculpted specifically for them. They talked and drank till the bar closed. As they were about to part, she reached up and gave him a kiss and said, "Anytime, Kamin, anytime. You have my number and you can reach me whenever you want."

The next morning Barnes was waiting for him. "I thought we had an understanding." Barnes barked.

Jesse was hung-over and was in no mood to banter with Barnes. "I can't do it any different than I'm doing."

Barnes walked over to Jesse's desk and said. "I'm getting a lot of heat because of this. The District Manager called me yesterday wanting to know what you are doing at Celex."

"Who is giving him all this heat?" Jesse asked.

"It's coming from Byrd's office and from a local congressman. These people have a lot of friends in high places and they are not above lying to get your ass."

"I don't give a damn what they do, 'cause I will do it right. Besides I think that the men at the mine are lying to the corporate people. If there is one thing that I have learned doing this job, it's that in large corporations one hand doesn't know what the other is doing." Jesse picked up his citation book and threw it to Barnes. "Take a look at that shit. I can't believe what I'm finding."

Barnes read the citations and finally looked up at Jesse. "Well, it's your ass, Kamin."

Jesse stayed in the office the rest of the day finishing all his paperwork. Barnes left the office early and was gone most of the day. After a couple of hours Jesse took a break and grabbed a cup of coffee and sat down in a chair in front of Chris Nolan's desk.

"Chris, you said that your husband worked at Celex for years. Was it always run so badly?"

"It's always had its problems, but the last six years have been real bad. I told you that my brother is still working there. He is always telling me stories about how things are going."

"What's your brother's name?"

"Jerry Ferrel. He runs the train load out."

"I haven't been there yet. I'll make a point of seeing him before I'm finished."

Chris said, "Now let's talk about something really important. How's your love life coming?" At that moment Booker walked in on them.

"Well?" She asked.

"I got girls falling all over me. Hell, I was with a good-looking brunette last night."

Booker slapped Jesse on the back and added. "We got us a briar patch jumper here." Chris started laughing so hard that Jesse thought she would fall out of her chair.

"Now settle down, Booker, one girl doesn't make a harem." Jesse said smiling.

Jesse walked back to his desk followed by Booker who was whistling a tune that Jesse recognized at once. He began to sing the words his mother had taught him so long ago. "*Step by step the longest march, can be won, can be won. Many stones can form an arch, singly none, singly none. And by union what we will can be accomplished still. Drops of water turn a mill, singly none, singly none.*"

Booker turned to him with a questioning look. "Where did you hear that song?"

Jesse looked up from his work answering. "My mom use to sing that to me when I was little, until I memorized the words. Why?"

Booker walked over to him. "My pa wrote that song. I wonder how your mom ever heard it. Pa never sold any of his songs. He told me that he wrote them for just my brothers and me."

Jesse said, "Every night at suppertime mom would have me pray to the two men that she said were our protectors. One was John L. Lewis and the other was Franklin Roosevelt. Then we would sing that song. The pictures of those two men are still hanging in my mom's dinning room." He stared into space with a dreamy distant look. "You know, my brother told me a story once about my Dad going to a UMW convention. He said that one of the guys got up to protest something Lewis said and before anyone could react two of Lewis's goons beat him so badly that they dragged his body out of the hall."

"Yeah," Booker replied. "Them were hard times."

"I have spent my life trying to learn the good and the bad of those times. I came to the conclusion that both Lewis and Roosevelt had dreams and they needed the misery of our people to make their dreams come true. The saddest thing I learned was that their actions caused a lot of that misery." He looked at Booker with pain in his eyes. "Ya know, Book, if I was to say that to my mom she would smack me across the face."

Booker sat down in front of Jesse shaking his head. "Kamin, the truth probably lies somewhere between your and your mom's vision of those times."

CHAPTER 44
I DON'T UNDERSTAND

The best way out of a difficulty is through it.

—Anonymous

The following morning Jesse returned to Celex. This time he was accompanied by Booker. Booker was to examine the training and all accident reports. Jesse chose to examine the draw off tunnels beneath the stockpiles of coal. He did not get far. He found coal spillage so deep that he could not get through. He was accompanied by Jared Davis and Jake Wyatt. He said to them both, "Well, gentleman, this is good as it gets. Did you think that I would not look in here? Tell you what, how 'bout I issue you an unwarrantable order for this little problem. Mr. Davis, now that I have issued this order you will receive orders on any future inspections for any violation that is unwarrantable no matter how serious it is. This facility will have to have a complete inspection without any violations that are unwarrantable to get out from under these kinds of orders." He returned to the mine office with the company hounds barking at his heels. He met with Booker who had barely started his work. It was going to be a long day.

The next day Jesse had two hours to work and he used most of that time talking with Chris Nolan. The rest of the men were out at various mines and Barnes was off.

"Chris, how did the guys let this place get so bad?"

She gave him a cynical look. "Come on, Jess, you been at it long enough to know that anytime an underground inspector gets a chance to work on the surface that it's vacation time. They are constantly taking heat from both sides and getting outside for a day really is a breather. I wouldn't blame them too much."

"I guess you're right. When I was underground, I didn't have the Union busting me from the time I got there till I went home. Ya know, when they first passed the Mining Act giving walkaround rights to the Union, I thought it was a good thing, but after seeing how they use it, as a weapon, I've changed my mind."

"I'll give you an example. The last inspection I was on before I came here I was at a Union surface mine. I was on the highwall one day and saw a dozer operator get out of his machine and take a fire extinguisher and break two windows in the cab. I hopped in my Jeep and drove around to where he was working. I flagged him down and told him I wanted to inspect the machine. Everything was perfect except the broken windows. He told me to put it to the company. I then told him that I saw him break the windows. I would have them fixed, but I would not write anything. His first words were "you going to tell". I kept my mouth shut 'cause I didn't want his family to suffer if he lost his job. That's the bullshit things our guys are dealing with." He paused and got a cup of coffee. "Hey, did I tell you that I have a date tomorrow with Beth Stewart?"

"At least three times. What is it about this girl that has you so riled up?"

"Chris, I have been trying to figure that out since I met her. I think in some ways she reminds me of my wife. She was as beautiful as Beth, she had blond hair, and she was as easy to talk to. It's been over twenty years since she died and I still miss her terribly. In all these years I have never attempted to get close to anyone. I don't know why I'm trying now."

Chris just rolled her eyes. "You're either horny or lonely, which is it?"

"Probably a little bit of both." He said sheepishly. He ended the conversation there. "Well, I have to go. I think I'll spend the rest of the day exploring. I want to bring my mother up next weekend and show her around."

"How old is your mom?" Chris asked.

"She is seventy-four and still one tough lady."

He walked out with a wave of his hand and no more thoughts of work.

CHAPTER 45
MUSIC AND GUNFIRE

There is no need hanging about for the Last Judgment - it takes place every day.

—Albert Camus, *The Fall*, 1956

On Saturday, the time dragged on so slowly that he thought something was wrong with the clock. The weather was nice, so he drove to Bradford Park, which was only a couple of miles away from the motel. Chris had told him about the place. He was able to walk around the lake. He even made it into Mt. Lake Park. He stumbled across F St. He walked all over that day. He really liked everything about Mt. Lake Park. He marveled at the large old Victorian homes, the heavily wooded streets and the quiet. It was very different from where he was raised. It finally was time to get ready, so he hurried back to his room.

He kept telling himself that a forty-four year old should not be acting like an eighteen year old on his first date. His logical self was losing to his fantasy. He was creating a new world in his mind.

He arrived at Beth's home right on time. He went to the door and knocked. He heard her moving around and then her footsteps on the stairwell. She opened the door and met him with a big smile. She was absolutely beautiful. Her blond hair was tied back in a ponytail. She was wearing jeans with boots, a sweater, and covered with a waist length leather jacket. He tried to relax and not act like an idiot.

"You're right on time. I like that." She said.

"And you didn't keep me waiting." He retorted.

The Legion hall was only a short ride away. They never stopped talking from the time they got into the car. The night was magical for both. Neither noticed the car that followed them to the Legion that night. His fantasy driven image was fulfilled and her brief escape from her suffocating life was euphoric.

The country band was very good and they danced almost every dance. Because of the noise they spent more time drinking beer than talking. The time went fast and the dance ended at 11:30. He helped her with her coat and they started to walk to his car. They were about the only ones who left that early. The rest stayed till closing time. They were about to the car when someone said, "I'd like to fuck that." Jesse turned and saw two very large men stepping from between two parked cars. Jesse pushed Beth away and turned to face them. "Listen, boys, if you're drunk I forgive you. If not get the hell away from us."

"What do you think, Buster, are we drunk or is it we just don't like assholes?" Said the largest of the two.

Jesse knew that if they made the first move he was done. He kicked as hard as he could, striking the closest man in the balls. It ended that one's will to fight. The other charged at Jesse whose reflexes were impaired by too much beer. Jesse was just a little too slow. The man drove him into a parked car cutting a large gash above his right eye stunning him. He could barely focus when he heard a loud crack. Then a voice said, "You make one move towards him and I'll put the next one in your head. I guarantee you that I won't miss from here." Jesse shook his head and realized that it was Beth doing the talking.

"Now pick up your friend and get out of here." There was no questioning her resolve. The man picked up his friend and moved away. "Get up, Jess."

"I didn't know that you had a gun on you." A surprised Jesse said.

"Honey, you're probably the only one in Garrett County not carrying one. That cut is pretty bad. We had better stop at the hospital." He started to argue with her but saw that it was no use. Five stitches later Jesse walked out into the waiting room of the hospital.

Beth smiled at him. "Honey, you look pretty good in black, blue, and white." She reached up and ran her hand over his bandaged face. She then gave him a delightful kiss.

He held her hand to his face. "I hope that our future dates aren't quite as eventful."

CHAPTER 46
SOME YOU WIN, SOME YOU LOSE

In a game, just losing is almost as satisfying as just winning. In life the loser's score is always zero.

—W. H. Auden, *"Postscript: The Frivolous and The Earnest," The Dyer's Hand*, 1962

Ralph Kolb was a little nervous about seeing Buck Storm. Mr. Storm was a man whom you did not disappoint.

Mrs. Storm answered the door.

"Hello, dear. William is in his study. You know the way."

"Thanks, Mrs. Storm. I only need a minute."

Kolb knocked on the study door.

He heard a rough, "Who is it?"

"It's Ralph, Mr. Storm."

"Well, Ralph, is that son-of-a-bitch hurting?"

"Things didn't go exactly as planned, Mr. Storm."

Storm's smile disappeared. "What happened?"

"Buster got hurt pretty bad and that woman he was with had a gun. I swear to God she would have killed me if I would have made a move towards that guy."

Storm thought for a minute finally saying, "This ain't over. Give it a month or so then come and see me."

CHAPTER 47
THE MALADY OF FRUSTRATION

Not to get what you have set your heart on is almost as bad as getting nothing at all.

—Aristotle, *Nicomachean Ethics (4th C. BC), 9.1,* TR. J. A. K. Thomson

Jesse got to the office early on Monday. Chris was the only one there. As soon as she saw him the questions began.

"What happened to you?" She quizzed.

"My date didn't go exactly as I planned."

Laughing, Chris said, "She did that to you?"

"Hell, no, a couple of drunks decided to pick a fight with me."

"Well, it appears that you lost."

"I would call it more of a draw."

Chris still smiling added. "All I've got to say is that it had better been worth it."

"It was." He smiled.

"I'm heading back to Celex. See you tomorrow."

When he arrived at the mine he found that the silo fire was out and contractors were working on the beltlines. He traveled to the refuse pile where all the mines waste material was stored. Three off road rock trucks were being used with another four tri-axle dump trucks. Within the hour he had all the trucks parked for one problem or another. Davis started to argue with him.

"We will have to shut the plant down if you park all those trucks."

Jesse answered coldly. "I don't give a damn if you ever run coal again."

The tone of the inspection was set that very first day. Jesse had always made a point of helping those who helped themselves. He had no mercy on anyone not trying to comply with the rules.

Wyatt, the Union representative, was just as angry as Davis. He saw Jesse as a threat to the livelihood of everyone. It did not dawn on him that he was partly responsible for this mess.

Jesse spent the entire week at the plant. He talked to every one of the workers. He explained what he had done and why. He sensed no animosity from the workers. It was more like indifference. On Friday, Davis informed him that all the work on the beltlines was completed.

Jesse said. "Let's check each one."

"You got to be kidding me." An angry Davis retorted.

"I have never been more serious."

They began the long process of going from belt to belt checking each emergency stop cord. Davis would call the plant operator and let him know that the belt would shut down and Jesse pulled each cord. Jesse was able to check all the guarding as well. After nearly four hours they were down to one beltline left to be examined. This belt carried coal from the raw coal stockpile to the top of the raw coal silo. This was the silo that had been on fire. The beltline was about four hundred feet long and climbed to the top of the silo approximately one hundred and fifty feet above the ground. Davis and Jesse walked up the beltline a distance of ten yards where Davis tripped the stop cord. The belt ran forward a few feet, stopped, and then reversed itself. Both men had to jump over the handrail to save themselves from being covered by the coal coming towards them.

"I can't believe this shit. You ain't got a brake on that belt!"

Davis apologetically said, "Believe me I wouldn't have pulled that cord if I had known."

"Let your superiors know that I am issuing another unwarrantable order for the brake on that beltline. The belt is down until you fix the condition and I lift the order."

It had been a long week and he was glad to get away from the mine.

CHAPTER 48
PLOTTING FRIENDS

What man knows is everywhere at war with what he wants.

—*Joseph Wood Krutch, "The Genesis of a Mood,"*
The Modern Temper, 1929

Jesse had been planning for his mother to come for the weekend, but late Friday he received a call from one of his sisters saying his mother was ill. It was nothing serious so he decided to stay in Oakland. He had not explored Deep Creek Lake yet so on Saturday he headed to the Wisp Ski Resort located at the lake. He liked the lake a lot. It had old cottages with a few businesses. He wondered how long it would take the world to discover this place.

He was sitting in the bar early that afternoon when he saw Beth Stewart and her friend Midge Rollins walk in. They did not see him so he decided to walk over and say hi. They both smiled and said hi at the same time.

"Hi, ladies, it is great to see both of you."

Before he could say another word Beth broke in. "I didn't know that you knew Midge." Then Midge spoke up.

"We met at the Starlite bar a few days ago." Turning to Jess, "What happened to you?"

He touched the bandage over his right eye. "I went out on a date." Beth began to laugh.

"He tried to open a car door with his head." Beth answered.

Midge sensed this was a private joke. She had known about the dance the week before, but Beth had not said anything about an accident.

"Are you ladies busy? This is my first time at the lake and I need someone to show me around."

Midge spoke first. "We were about to have lunch. Would you like to join us?" Beth shot her a quick glance. It was not like Midge to be so enthusiastic about a guy that Beth had expressed an interest in.

Jesse was oblivious to Midge's flirting. He was consumed with thoughts of Beth. Each time that he tried to corner her Midge would interrupt them. They spent about three hours together. It had been pleasant for all three. As the women were walking to their car, Jesse yelled out to Beth. "Can I talk to you for a moment?"

She walked back to him while Midge got the car. "What do you need?"

Jesse stumbled for a moment. "It's, ah, it's just that I don't have your telephone number. Would you share it with me?"

"Sure," she smiled. "But it's in the phone book. The number is 334-1102. Give me a call whenever. I like to talk."

He watched as they drove away. He walked back into the bar pulling his wallet out. He found a piece of paper and wrote Beth's number on it. As he started to put the paper back, he noticed that he had written the number on the same paper that Midge had used for her phone number. I am going to have to watch that, he thought.

CHAPTER 49
THE NEVER ENDING INSPECTION

Man is his own worst enemy.

—Cicero

He got to the office early and found Chris hard at it.

"How was your visit with your mom?" Chris asked.

"She wasn't able to come out so I wandered around the Lake on Saturday."

"You better watch that place; you'll get into trouble there."

"As a matter of fact I had lunch with two beautiful ladies."

Again Booker walked in at the tail end of a conversation. "Two women at one time. You got me worried, Kamin."

"Booker, it was lunch not sex." Jesse answered shaking his head.

Chris asked, "Who were the girls?"

"Beth Stewart and Midge Rollins. Do you know Midge?"

"I know both of them. Beth is about your speed, but you had better watch Rollins. She goes through men faster than Booker can go through that there Bible."

Booker chimed in with, "Amen."

"I can take care of myself." Jesse said.

Chris shook her head and stared at his eye. "I see how you can take care of yourself."

Getting tired of the talk Jesse got up. "One of us has got to earn our wages. I'm heading back to Celex. I should finish this week." Turning to Booker, he added. "Want to come along?"

"Can't. I got to go to Morgantown. Big meeting this morning. You stirred up a hornet's nest. Storm and Celex are raising holy hell. You're probably the only one that ain't invited. Nobody is happy with you right now."

Chris stood up getting another cup of coffee and to light her eighth cigarette of the day. "Listen, big guy, you had better be watching your ass. It is easy to get thrown to the wolves especially when big brother does the throwing."

"I'll watch myself, I promise." Answering as he gathered up his gear. "See you all later."

His spirits were high as he drove to the mine. He gave little thought to the meeting Booker mentioned. Instead he thought of Beth. The more he spoke to her the better he liked her. He had been fantasizing about her from the very first time he saw her. It still puzzled him why he cared so much about someone he had just met, but he did.

Davis and Wyatt were waiting for him. He only had the train load out and the rail siding to do. He thought it should be an easy day. The three of them used his Ram Charger to drive over to the load out. He parked right in front of a shanty used by the car droppers. They were just getting out of his vehicle when four loaded coal cars being dropped out derailed right in front of them. The two car droppers were wearing safety belts and were not thrown from the loads. Jesse thought to himself, I bet the only reason they are wearing them belts is because I'm here.

When he and the rest had walked over to see what had caused the derailment, they found the fish plates that held the rails together were not bolted.

Jesse asked, "Can you guys get me a couple cans of fluorescent spray paint?"

Davis said, "What do you need that for?"

"We are going to walk the track and mark the locations of problems. That way when you get hold of the railroad, you won't have to be here to show them what is needed."

There were eight sets of tracks for loaded and empty cars. As he walked the tracks he understood why there were so many cars lying in that ditch. He found many fish plates that were not bolted. There were ties so rotted that he could pull the spikes from them by hand. He measured the distance between the rails and found many out of gauge—the distance was too great. The derail switch that prevented loaded cars from accidentally rolling onto the main line was damaged and would not work. Finally he turned to Davis.

"Mr. Davis, I am issuing you a citation that will take the track out of service until it is repaired."

"Shit! That shuts us down again. This is a bunch of bullshit. We have been using that track for years."

"I don't give a damn. You're going to get someone killed if you don't start doing it right."

Davis walked away mumbling, "What an asshole."

Wyatt never said a word. He was as upset with Kamin as Davis, but not for the same reason. Where Davis was worried about telling the corporate people, Wyatt was worried about his next paycheck.

Jesse talked to the car droppers and went up the steps to the load out. He entered the load out operator's room.

"My name's Jerry Ferrel." The load out operator said.

"Ah, your Chris's brother." Jesse answered.

"Yeah, she said to keep an eye on you and to give you a hand if I could. I'm glad you're doing something with that track. I've been worried that someone would get killed on that damn thing."

"Yeah, I can't believe how bad a shape it's in. In fact, I can't believe how much of a mess the whole place is." Jess said.

Ferrel shrugged, "It's taken a while to get this way. Hey, while you're here could you get them to do something with that retarder? It hasn't worked in weeks."

The retarder allowed the load out operator to drop the cars through while being loaded. It was a winch with a cable that hooked to the rail cars and allowed the load out operator to control the speed of the cars. When he had finished loading the cars, they would disconnect the cable. Then the car droppers would take the cars.

"Yeah, when I go back down I'll check it out."

Ferrel gave Jesse a brief history of the plant. "I don't want you to get the wrong idea. There are a lot of good people here. It's just been run badly. I'm going to tell you a story about Chris and this plant. When my brother-in-law had his heart attack, they didn't have any money coming in. The guys and the night boss fixed it so Chris could work in his place, outside with the rest of us. She was here every night for nearly a year. They got their paycheck and survived. Not one guy or that boss ever said a word."

Jesse stood there with his mouth open. "That was some story. It's hard to believe that they got away with it for a year."

"Ya know what the worst part was? My brother-in-law had over thirty years in the Union and because he died so young Chris never got a damn penny. That's why she's working with you today."

Davis interrupted them. "I got a hold of the track superintendent. He's sending a crew over."

"OK, I'll give you all the time you need to take care of everything. When they get those fish plates bolted and get some good ties in I'll allow the guys to use the track while they finish the work."

Jesse used the remainder of the day checking the water treatment plant and a small shop used for welding and maintenance.

When he got back to the office he found Chris and Booker still at it. Booker jumped up when he came in. "You was real popular at that meeting. You got everybody upset. The District Manager was even there."

"What's got them so upset, Booker?"

"'Cause you're making waves. They don't want to be getting calls from congressman and senators."

"I don't understand. What did they think I should have done?" A perplexed Jesse answered.

"They wanted you to come and talk to them first. You embarrassed them. They ain't happy."

"I guess they're going to have to get happy all over again."

Chris chimed in, "You've made so many friends since you came here that I would be afraid to go out at night."

Jesse turned to her. "You're exaggerating."

"Yeah, I can tell that every time I look at that cut over your eye."

Jesse laughed, "That had nothing to do with my job. Let's skip it."

Chris stared at him as he walked back to his desk. Booker was also worried about Kamin.

CHAPTER 50
YOU DON'T CONTROL ME

There are some things the arrogant mind does not see; it is blinded by its vision of what it desires.

—Wendell Berry, *"People, Land, and Community," Standing by Words*, 1983

The following day Jesse returned to the plant. When he arrived, he was met by a smiling Davis.

"Where's Wyatt?" Jesse asked.

"He had a doctor's appointment today. He figured that you had covered everything and you wouldn't need a walk-around. Besides I wanted to let you know that the railroad finished that work you wanted them to do. They came in on the afternoon shift."

Jesse was shocked. "Do you mean that they got all that work done? How many guys did they bring in? What do you say we go check it out?"

They drove Jesse's car to the siding. It was a bright sunny day and unusually warm for this time of the year. Jesse was in a surprisingly good mood. This was all he had to do to finish this inspection. But the mood did not last long. As he and Davis checked the track, he quickly found out how the railroad was able to do so much work in such a short time.

"Look at this." Jesse said.

He reached down and pulled two new spikes from a rotted tie. At every location that he had marked all that was done was cosmetic. Rails that were out of gauge were barred over until they were at the right distance but the rotted ties were not replaced. Most of the fish plates were left unbolted. The only thing actually fixed was the de-rail switch.

A very frustrated Jesse turned to Davis. "Call that track superintendent for this area. I want to see him."

Davis, annoyed that Jesse had been so meticulous, said, "It will take a while for him to get over here. That is if he can at all."

"Tell him I am going to have a Federal Track Inspector here in the morning. That should make up his mind."

They waited three hours for the supervisor to show up. He came in a brand new pickup and when Jesse saw the man in spotless attire with a hardhat that also appeared new. He thought, this guy does not get out much. The man was taller than Jesse and well built. He had a smile as he came up to them and introduced himself.

"The name is Sabo. What's the problem?"

Jesse began, "You had a crew in here last night to work on this siding. They didn't do the work."

The man's smile suddenly vanished. "You don't know what the hell you're talking about, mister."

Jesse started to get angry but held his temper. "I specifically marked each problem for the crew to repair. The work wasn't done."

"It meets the standards for rail sidings." The man bellowed.

Trying to be reasonable, Jesse said. "The track is unsafe in its present condition. How much time do you need to get all the work done?"

Sabo turned to Davis. "This son-of-a-bitch has no authority over us."

Before Davis could respond Jesse broke in. "He's

right. I have no authority over the railroad. I am issuing the mine an order on the track. I don't give a shit if you ever use it." He left both men standing there and returned to his car. He began to write the order. Davis stayed away from him while he worked.

When Jesse had finished, he took the paper work to Davis.

"You really pissed that guy off." Davis interjected.

"I really don't give a damn. He comes in here trying to intimidate me. I don't do intimidation well. This is between you and the railroad. Call me and let me know what you decide."

When Jesse got to the office he found Chris waiting for him.

"What the hell did you do out there?"

"Why?" Jesse asked.

"Because Barnes has been on the phone most of the day with Celex, the district, and the railroad."

"I shut the siding down at the plant."

"Well, you sure stirred up a hornet's nest. You're going to get nailed as soon as he finds out you're here."

The phone rang. Chris answered the call. "It's for you. Mr. Davis."

Jesse walked back to his desk and took the call.

"Kamin."

"Mr. Kamin, the railroad has decided to fix the siding. They say that it will take two days."

"OK, let's set up a closeout conference for Thursday at 9:00 AM."

Jesse slipped out of the office while Barnes was still on the phone. He did not feel like arguing with him too. He was walking to his car when he spotted Beth. He tried to get her attention but she kept right on going.

233

CHAPTER 51
THE CLOSEOUT

Don't stand shivering upon the bank; plunge in at once and get it over.

—Thomas Chandler Haliburton

On Thursday Jesse headed to Celex for his closeout conference. He was accompanied by Barnes, who had insisted on coming along. They arrived early so Jesse could check out the repairs to the rail siding. He finished writing the termination for the order he had issued.

He then entered the office. The conference room was large. It had a very long and wide table that could have seated twenty. At one end was the mine superintendent. To Jesse's left sat Wyatt and three members of the Union safety committee. To his right sat Davis, the plant foreman, and Barnes. Barnes would not even sit with him. They purposely had isolated him. He now sat at the end of the table far away from everyone.

Jesse began, "First, are there any questions?" He no sooner got the words out of his mouth when Davis stood up holding the wad of papers that Jesse had written.

"I want to talk about these." He said.

"If you want to talk about any of those citations and orders I would suggest you call the District office. I have no more to say about them." Jesse responded. "This meeting is about preventing this from happening in the future." Again he was interrupted. They all began talking at once and they were all attacking him. Barnes sat there and never said a word. Finally Jesse cut them off.

"It took the Union, the company, and the government to get you in this shape. It ends now. If you have anymore to say you can say it to him." He pointed to Barnes and then walked out.

CHAPTER 52
MINDLESS MEN

That is the nature of women, not to love when we love them, and to love when we love them not.

—Miguel de Cervantes, *Don Quixote (1605-15) 1.3.6,* TR. *John Ozell*

It had been two weeks since his now infamous closeout conference with Celex Coal. Barnes was still treating him coolly and he expected more grief to follow. He had visited several mines and found the people interesting. Most were hard working and tried to do things right. It had been his luck to visit the two worst jobs in the mountains first. If it were not for Celex and Storm, this would be a great place to work.

Today was the first really big snowfall that he had experienced since coming to Oakland. They had gotten twelve inches and it still was snowing hard. He and Booker had gone out together that morning. Traveling on Route 560, they came to a long turn with broad meadows on each side of the road. All of a sudden Jesse could not see. It was a wall of white. He took his foot off the gas not knowing what else to do. He spied a car beside him just inches away. To say that it scared him was an understatement. He somehow stayed on the road and as abruptly as it began the wind subsided. Shaken, he and Booker just stared at one another.

Booker said, "Kamin, you are sure lucky that you had me come along."

"Why's that?"

"'Cause it's the next thing to having the Lord with you."

"Jesus, Booker, you are one hell of a preacher."

"Don't be swearing, you hear."

"How much further do we have to go, Booker?"

"It's about three more miles to Kilbert Strip."

Jesse did not expect to find anyone working, but to his surprise they found Mr. Kilbert and his two sons hard at it. They were all three on bulldozers. Jesse checked out the equipment and everything else. Not finding any problems, he asked Mr. Kilbert if he could see all of his records. Mr. Kilbert said, "My wife use to take care of everything but she passed away a few months ago. I think everything is OK though."

Jesse glanced at the paperwork and it appeared in order. By the time he returned to Oakland the snow had let up. "You know, Booker. The more time I spend here the better I like it. For the most part the people are great."

Booker smiled. "People are nice most everywhere, if you take the time to know them."

When they got back to the office they found that everyone had called off because of the weather, except Chris and them. They put their gear away and came back into Chris's office to have a cup of coffee.

Chris said, "Deer season is coming up. Why don't you take some time off and hunt with me and my boy? I got about a hundred and fifty acres on my place and we have a dozen rifles."

Jesse was excited. "That sounds like fun. I haven't been hunting since my brother died. We hunted and fished year round."

Laughing, Booker chimed in, "Do you really want to put a lethal weapon in the hands of this troublemaker?

He's got enough people mad at him now. Them deer had better watch out 'cause he takes no prisoners."

Jesse acted stunned, "I promise to take only one."

Jesse was able to make it back to the motel, but barely. The snow had gotten worse. He decided to call Beth and see if she would go out that weekend.

Beth: "Hi."

Jesse: "Would you like to go out to dinner on Saturday?"

Beth: "Sure, if you let me pick the place and treat you."

Jesse: "Sure, what do you have in mind?"

Beth: "Let's try the Cornish Manor. I heard that it's great."

They talked for over an hour. She mentioned her work; they talked about the weather, and things of mutual interest. But nothing personal was brought up by either of them.

Jesse lit up whenever he talked to her. His mind was working strangely. He was placing her so high that she was becoming untouchable. It was as if she were better than all other women. He gave her near saintly status. He was becoming obsessed with her. The strange part was that he was not conscious of doing so.

On Saturday evening Beth was rushing to get ready for her date when the phone rang. It was Midge.

Midge: "Honey, I just wanted you to know before you read it in the papers."

Beth: "Know what?"

Midge: "That ex-husband of yours just got arrested for passing a bad check."

Beth never answered her. She just hung up the phone and began crying. No matter what she did she could not escape the jeers and snide comments that followed her because of that man. She had made up her mind to succeed. No matter what the price. She would make all those hypocrites squirm. Then the doorbell rang.

An unenthusiastic hi greeted Jesse.

"Is there something wrong?" Jesse said with concern.

"This is just what I need right now, to be out with a man." Beth moaned.

They rode to the restaurant in near silence. Other than to give Jesse directions little else was said.

After they were seated, Jesse tried to brighten her mood.

"I'm going to take off a couple of days after Thanksgiving. Chris Nolan has invited me to hunt with her and her boy."

Before he could say more, "You hunt?" A decidedly upset Beth asked.

"Sure, I really enjoy it." Jesse quietly said.

What he did not know was that this had caused great arguments between Beth and her former husband. He abandoned her for long periods of time. He was always going somewhere to hunt or fish.

Jesse did not understand what was happening. He thought she was acting like some Jekyll and Hyde.

They ate quickly and Beth said, "I would like to go home."

In the car things got worse. Jesse made a flippant remark that really set Beth off.

"Let me tell you, I don't need a man telling me anything. I'm not about to spend my life washing a man's underwear or being a slave to anything else he wishes."

When they pulled up to her house, Jesse tried one more time.

"I don't know what's wrong, but I care for you, Beth."

Beth was beyond words. Her anger would not allow her to reason. She opened the door and left without a word.

Jesse was so angry he became unreasonable with everyone. He tried calling Beth several times over the next few days. She would not answer. He finally out of desperation waited for her at her house. She came home near ten that night. She did not see him until he called her name. He saw the look on her face. She had rolled her eyes when she turned to face him.

"Beth, I don't know what's bothering you, but I want you to know that I care very deeply about you."

"Jess, you're a nice guy but I'm not ready for a relationship, with you or anyone."

"Damn it, Beth, I'm in love with you."

"I don't want anybody to love me, you understand." With that she turned and walked away.

Jesse went home for Thanksgiving to visit his family. They could all sense that something was wrong, but Jesse was not talking. He spent two days in Adena. He told his mother that he had to get back to Oakland, to get things ready for work on that Monday. It was a lie. He just wanted to be alone.

Monday morning found him at Chris Nolan's home. They were standing in her rec room where she offered him a rifle for the hunt. It was just breaking daylight when she made a quick move for her rifle. It was leaning up against the wall. She slid open the sliding glass doors and stepped onto her deck. Without a word she brought the rifle up to her shoulder and fired.

"Now that's the way I like to hunt." She laughed.

Jesse went outside and found a ten-point buck lying

only thirty feet away. She had busted that buck and had not even left the comfort of her home.

He hunted for the two days and never even got a shot. What was even worse? It rained for the entire time.

When he returned to work he was moody and sullen. He talked very little and made sure he did not return to the office until everyone had left. This went on for over two weeks until finally there was a note from Barnes; see me tomorrow, it read.

He got into the office early and as usual he found Chris and Booker having coffee and gossiping.

Chris was the first to speak. "Where have you been, Kamin? We were about to go hunting you ourselves."

"I've been working. Why?"

"Everyone has been asking for you."

"Like who?"

"Well, that Beth Stewart for one." This got Jesse's attention immediately.

"You say she came here looking for me. What did you tell her?"

Chris smiled, amused. "I said I would let you know. Hey, what are you smiling about?"

"I knew that she couldn't stay away forever."

He started to whistle and waked back to his desk. He spied the note and yelled back. "Hey, Chris, do you know why Barnes wants to see me?"

"No, why?"

"Well I better make a short day of it." Jesse then said to Booker. "Booker, I'm going to do a spot inspection of Storm's job. You want to go with me?"

"Can't. I have to go to Morgantown this morning."

"You spend more time in that office than the district manager does." Jesse grabbed his gear and headed out the door.

CHAPTER 53
THE LAST STRAW

Men often make up in wrath what they want in reason.

—W. R. Alger

It took him about fifty minutes to get to Storm's job. It had been many weeks since his first visit and he figured that the stories about Storm were exaggerated. If he was as bad as they say, something would have happened long before this.

He met Bart Kolb as soon as he arrived. "Tell Mr. Storm that I am here. I am going to do a spot inspection."

"Buck ain't here. He went into Cumberland."

"As long as you know, that's all I need." Jesse then walked over to where two men were working on a Caterpillar D9 dozer. He talked to them for a while, letting them know about recent accidents that he was aware of. He then spied a Terex rock truck coming out of the pit. He got into position to get the driver's attention and flagged him down. The man geared the truck down and turned the truck's wheels into a bank of dirt. Jesse knew that something was wrong immediately.

Jesse yelled up to the driver. "How about staying in the cab? I want to check the machine out."

The driver said, "What's your name again?"

"The name's Jesse Kamin. Now move away from that dirt. I want to check your steering."

The driver did as he was instructed. Jesse found

the steering to be in good repair. "Now pull forward and try your brakes." The driver did what he was told and pulled forward. When he hit the brakes the truck began moving faster. Fortunately he was able to steer the machine back into the bank of dirt stopping it.

A shocked Jesse ran over to the truck. "Why the hell didn't you tell me that the brakes don't work?"

"Mister, around here you get fired for opening your mouth."

Jesse walked over to Kolb. "I'm shutting down that truck. It doesn't have any brakes."

Kolb stuttered, "I'll have to ask Buck."

"I'm not asking him anything. I'm telling you that the truck is down until the brakes are fixed."

Jesse checked seven machines that day and wrote three orders. He had shut down two trucks and an end loader. While he was writing the orders Storm came barreling into the pit. Before his truck had completely stopped, he was out of it, yelling. "What the hell is going on here? Why are those machines parked?"

Jesse got out of the car with the orders in hand and approached Storm. "I had them park those machines. They ain't safe to run."

"Why, you big feeling son-of-a-bitch. You're lucky you don't work for me."

"You're right, I don't work for you. I work for them." He pointed towards Storm's men. He tried to hand the papers to Storm who jerked them out of his hands.

Storm was furious. "You can shove them papers up your ass!" And with a flick of his wrist he sent the papers flying into the air. The wind blew them all over the pit.

Jesse said, "Storm, give me a call when you got them fixed. Just don't move them till I get back here and check them." Both Jesse and Storm would have gone at each other if it was not for Kolb getting between them.

When Jesse arrived at the office he found Barnes waiting for him. "It's about time you got back here."

Jesse's mood was ugly. He was not about to take crap from Barnes. "I had trouble with Storm. I want to talk to you about it."

Barnes was holding some kind of paper. "I need you to do something about this first."

"What is it?" Jesse asked.

"It's a bath house waiver. It's way overdue." He handed the papers to Jesse.

"A bath house waiver! I'm telling you that someone is going to get killed at that guy Storm's and you're pissing with a bath house waiver."

Barnes was not impressed. "If it's that bad at Storm's tell his men to go find another job, 'cause you can't be there every day."

Jesse was out of control. Chris heard the yelling from her desk and came to see what was going on.

"Let's talk about the real world. There ain't any jobs. These men are going to do what they have to." Jesse fumed.

"You heard me. I want this waiver taken care of right now! I don't want the district hounding me anymore."

Jesse was beside himself. "What a fucking crock!" He turned and nearly knocked Chris down leaving.

He got into his car and headed out. He pulled into a bar not far from the office. He needed a drink. He was surprised to find Beth Stewart sitting alone, nursing a beer. He walked over to her.

"You mind if I join you?" He quickly became aware that she was not smiling.

She stared up at him. "I wanted to talk to you anyway."

"Chris told me that you had stopped in at the office looking for me."

"Yeah, I wanted to tell you that I think it's best if we don't see each other anymore."

"What?"

Beth dropped her eyes. "We aren't looking for the same things. You want a wife and I don't want a husband. There are things I have to do and you would only complicate them. You're a nice guy, Jess, but I'm just not interested."

He watched her leave and ordered another beer. He sat there for over an hour. His mood varied from anger to heartbreak. He was about to leave when Chris Nolan came walking in.

"I figured I would find you in one of these bars."

Jesse barely looked at her. "What ya need?"

"Barnes is really angry. He's threatening to have you fired."

"Huh, if there's one thing I know about the government. It's harder to get fired than promoted. The last time I saw them try to fire a guy, they ended up paying through the nose. He still has his job. Anyway Barnes ain't stupid. He knows that if he goes down that road he would have a lot of explaining to do. Incidentally that guy I told you they tried to fire, he's a supervisor now."

He watched as Chris's eyes began to follow something.

"What are you looking at?"

"You see that guy that just came in?"

Jesse glanced up and saw a man with blond hair, and a build similar to his. "Yeah. What about him?"

"That's your honey's ex."

This time Jesse eyed him with interest. "He doesn't mean anything to me."

"Just thought you would want to know. Anyway, I did want to warn you about Barnes. One more thing: do you have my home number?"

"Nope."

She grabbed a napkin and wrote her telephone number on it.

"Just in case you need to talk." She got up and started to leave and then turned to him.

"Jess, you're too good for that girl. You're getting in way over your head. Just be careful."

"Thanks, Chris. I'll see you tomorrow."

He continued to drink for hours. Finally he decided to go back to his room. As he was walking out, the man that Chris told him was Beth's former husband stood up and blocked him, with a hand to Jesse's chest.

"The name's Stewart, Michael Stewart. I hear that you have been fucking my property." The words were so slurred that at first Jesse did not quite understand.

"Take your hand off me, Mister." Jesse was in such a foul mood that if the man had been sober, he would have seen the anger in Jesse's eyes. Instead, he pushed Jesse backwards. Jesse drove his fist into the man's nose. It got worse from there. Three men pulled Jesse off Stewart. The third man, the bartender, had a short piece of pipe that finally ended Jesse's rage.

At 3:00 AM Jesse was led from a cell in the Sheriff's office to an outer room where Chris Nolan was waiting.

"This lady posted your bail. I would suggest that you give up drinking. It appears that you can't handle it." The rotund Sheriff's deputy then turned to Chris. "He's all yours."

Chris walked out of the courthouse without looking at Jesse. She never volunteered a word. When they got into the car Jesse was the first to speak.

"I'm sorry, Chris."

She looked at him with disgust. "They said that you broke that man's jaw and two of his ribs. I thought I knew you, but I don't."

"Chris, he pushed me and said something about Beth. It was as if a bomb went off in me. I couldn't stop myself."

Chris was not buying his excuse. "Remember our discussion about Barnes? You just gave him the ammunition to get rid of you."

"Do you remember my story about them trying to fire someone? If it had been Barnes that I beat up, maybe. I don't even think that they will question me about this."

Chris glanced at him and saw that humorless grin and decided it was no use in pursuing the conversation. She pulled up to his room at the motel and Jesse got out. His only comment was "thanks".

CHAPTER 54
FRIENDS AND ENEMIES

Lord what fools these mortals be!

—William Shakespeare, *A Midsummer Night's Dream (1595-1596), 3.2. 115*

The following day was Saturday and Jesse did not come out of his room till late afternoon. He did not go to the restaurant; he headed straight to the bar. He was there for about an hour when he saw Beth come through the door. The look of rage in her eyes sobered him quickly. She walked right up to him.

"How could you have done that to Michael?" He had no chance to respond. "I don't want you to ever come near me again."

Jesse had been drinking too much and did not give a damn what he said.

"He's an asshole."

She was still livid. "He was drunk."

No matter how much he cared for her, he could not stop himself from making it worse. When she turned and walked away he knew that whatever chance he had with her was gone.

He sat at the bar for hours drinking and fuming, trying to rationalize what he had done. It was something how a mind can justify the most heinous actions that a man can commit. Then he would think of Beth. She was his only regret. He did not even notice the pretty brunette sit down beside him.

"Hi, big guy."

It was Midge Rollins, Beth's friend.

He limply smiled. "Hi."

Midge had just come from talking with Beth. She was well aware of what had occurred. It was just the opportunity that she had been waiting for.

They made small talk for over an hour. The music started. The bar had a small room where couples could dance. A DJ would come in on Saturday nights and spin records. Midge tried to coax him onto the dance floor. Jesse was not quite ready for that. Neither one had brought up Beth or Michael. Midge was persistent and finally she dragged Jesse to his feet. The DJ played several country songs that were easy to dance to. Finally, he played a slow song. As quick as the music started Midge slid her hand inside the back of his pants and said, "I think you could use a friend tonight." Without a word he led her to the door. Lust was about to overcome reason.

That same night, Buck Storm sat in his den. He was deep in thought. He wanted his punishment of Jesse Kamin to be memorable, so much so that no other son-of-a-bitch would have the balls to bother him again. He was about to call Ralph Kolb when his son burst in. The boy always made Buck's day. He was tall, blond, well built, and had a good mind.

"Hey, Dad, can I get a couple of bucks from you?"

"Tell you what, Bill. If you come out to the job for your break from school I'll give you a thousand dollars. What ya say?"

"You got a deal. I could sure use the money."

"Here's fifty, go and have a good time. But tomorrow you go to the job with me."

"You got it, Dad, thanks. "

Buck watched him leave. With a smile on his face, he thought, that boy is the only thing I love in this world. He then turned back to business.

CHAPTER 55
THE CALM BEFORE THE STORM

It is a good thing to learn caution by the misfortunes of others.

—Publilius Syrus

HOT SPOTS HAMPER UTAH MINE RESCUE

—*Wheeling News-Register*, November 21, 1984

Jesse came to work that Monday expecting Barnes to jump all over him. He was surprised to find that Barnes had taken leave for the entire week. A sister in Kentucky was ill.

"Hey, Chris, Barnes put this bath house waiver problem on my desk. It's for Kilbert Strip. I was just there and Mr. Kilbert told me his wife passed away a few months ago. He also said she took care of all the paperwork. I'm guessing that this got overlooked during that time. I've got an idea. How about typing out a waiver form for them and date it for June the sixth, eighty-four. I'll stick around till you finish and take it out and have them sign it."

"I'll have it ready in a few minutes. Ya know, I don't understand why we waste time on these anyway."

Jesse got back to the office around one. He walked straight into Chris's office and copied the wavier form that had been signed by Kilbert and his sons. He gave Chris the original.

"Chris, how about mailing this back to them? I'll attach the copy to this request for action form and put it on Barnes's desk, end of problem."

"You're just lucky. I like you." She said laughing. She stared up at him again. "Why the long face after doing such a good deed?"

He came over and sat in front of her desk. "I did something stupid."

"What stupid thing was that? Like beating that man or was there some other stupid thing you did?"

"Give me a break. After you let me off, I spent the day drinking at the Starlite. Beth ended up coming into the bar late that afternoon. She told me she never wanted to see me again. I kept on drinking. At about 7:30 that night her friend Midge walked in and before I knew it."

Chris was not surprised. "You don't have to say more. I got the picture. You ended up sleeping with her." Jesse just nodded. "You idiot, I warned you about her. She wears notches on her girdle like a man does on his belt."

They had not noticed Booker walk in, until he said. "Is our briar patch jumper at it again?"

Jesse turned, "I'm in no mood for jokes, Booker."

Chris chimed in, "He's not only a briar patch jumper, he does it while playing blind man's bluff." Booker started to laugh hysterically. Seeing he was not going to get any sympathy, Jesse walked out.

He did not see anyone the following day. He came into the office long before the others arrived and gathered his things. He did not come back until they were all gone. He did this again the following day. He did not want to talk to anyone. He had tried to contact Beth several times but she would not answer his calls.

Chris had left him a note saying that Midge had called him. He chose not to return hers. What a mess, he thought. One girl he loved would have nothing to do with him and another girl he used would not let him alone.

On Thursday he came into the office to find everyone gathered around Chris's desk. They were listening to the news.

"Twenty-seven men trapped by a fire that is hampering rescue operations." The radio announcer said.

"Where did that happen at?" Jesse asked.

Chris was the one to answer. "It's a mine in Utah. The name is Wilberg."

Frank Carter said, "Several men from up here went to work for that outfit only a few months ago. We're waiting to hear if any of them are among the ones trapped."

Arney Smith jumped in. "I'm sure glad I wasn't inspecting that mine. Them boys are screwed."

Chris wanted to know. "What does that mean?"

Jesse answered her. "Shit rolls downhill. That means the lowest guy on the totem pole is going to get hung. Government is into protecting power, not telling the truth. They will serve up a token to satisfy the public and the press. Arney is right; thank God it's not us."

They went about their work but all were glued to the radio or television that day.

When he came in on Friday, Chris asked. "You staying for the holidays, Jess?"

"Yeah, my mom is going out to my sister's again. I've decided to take off some time in January. We are all going to get together for a weekend at Mom's place to celebrate the holidays then."

Chris offered him a cup of coffee that she had just poured. "Why don't you come to my place on Christmas Eve? Every year a bunch of us get together. You would meet a lot of nice people. Maybe it would cheer you up."

"Let me think about it, Chris. I'll let you know next week." With that he was gone.

He was out early on that Friday and did not return to the office until two in the afternoon. Chris heard him enter the office. She walked over to him. "I'm glad that you came in before I left."

"Is something wrong?" A worried Jesse asked.

"No, Beth Stewart left a message for you. She wants you to meet her at the Bet-Mar restaurant, at four. She sounded strange."

Excited, Jesse said, "Thanks for telling me. I am going to stay in the office on Monday. No sense starting anything on Christmas Eve."

"Barnes just called me. He won't be back until after Christmas." Chris said.

"Well, that was a nice early Christmas present," Jesse said, as he walked back to his desk. He dumping his gear and yelled, "See you Monday."

His thoughts were filled with fantasy. Was she sorry about what she had said to him? Did she realize that she loved him? Did Midge tell her about the night they spent together? His mind was whirling.

The time dragged as it approached four. He drove to the restaurant pulling into the parking lot at exactly four. He parked and walked to the front door. He did not notice a car parked at the far end of the lot. Three men were in the car watching. He went into the restaurant, but Beth was not there. He waited for ten minutes and then walked back to the car. He could not understand. Why would she call him and then not show up? He waited for another ten minutes then he finally drove away.

The three men in the car were Buck Storm, Ralph Kolb, and a large man nicknamed Bull. After Jesse left, they exited the car and went inside. They were there just a short time when another man walked in.

"Hi, Uncle Buck."

"Mike, you sure look like shit." Michael Stewart's face was swollen, black, and blue from the beating Jesse had given him.

Buck said, "Sit down. We were just discussing our problem. Did you see him leave? By the way, your friend Midge did good. We may need her again." Turning to the other men, Storm said, "Kamin thought he was meeting his girlfriend thanks to her."

Michael said, "Midge and I are buddies. She has no idea that I have been using her. She placed that call for me just to get even with that guy." Buck just grunted acknowledgement. "By the way, Uncle Buck. You had better send enough men. He ain't no slouch." Michael looked at the big man. "I want him hurt real good. I want him hurt so bad that it takes him months to recover, not weeks."

Storm interrupted him. "Ralph, you and Bull take two additional guys with you. Make sure he doesn't see your faces." Smiling at all three, Buck said, "I think Christmas Eve would be the perfect time."

CHAPTER 56
TO LIVE OR DIE

Every man is the architect of his own fortunes.

—Sallust

Monday, Christmas Eve, found Chris and Jesse alone in the office. Everyone else had taken annual leave.

"So she never showed up?" Chris asked.

"No, I waited for a long time and finally left. I tried calling after I got home, but there was no answer."

"That's strange, 'cause she said she was anxious to see you."

Jesse was really down, "I don't know what the hell is going on. I think I'll just leave her alone for a few weeks. I'll try to contact her after the holidays."

"You still haven't given me an answer about tonight." Chris drilled.

"I guess I'll come. I just don't feel like being alone."

"Good, you will have fun in spite of yourself." At that moment the phone rang.

"MSHA," Chris answered.

"That's great, Merry Christmas." She hung up the phone, with a big grin on her face.

"What are you grinning about?"

"That was the District. They said close the office at noon, and wished us a Merry Christmas."

"What time do you want me at your place?" Jesse asked.

"I told everyone to be there at 7:30. Why don't you get out of here? I'll close up."

"I'm getting hungry. I think I'll stop at the Ranch bar. See you tonight."

At around 4:00 that afternoon Chris found she needed a couple things for the party, so she drove into town. As she was passing the Ranch, she saw Jesse's car was still there. She swung in.

She found him nursing a beer. Surprisingly there were two others sitting at a table beside him.

"What are you still doing here?" Chris asked.

"I didn't feel like going back to the motel. This is as good a place as any to kill some time."

She began to talk, but Jesse was not paying attention. He was listening to the two fellows sitting at the next table.

One asked. "You found a job yet?"

The other said, "Nah, I'm going to wait till the unemployment runs out, then I'll start looking."

"Hey, Kamin, are you listening to me?" As she spoke the men got up and left.

"I was listening to that conversation behind us. One man was telling the other he would not look for work till his unemployment ran out. It reminded me of my hometown. A recession and the EPA made beggars out of a lot of good men. I hope it doesn't happen here."

Jesse began to smile.

"What's so funny?" Chris snapped.

"I had a dream once. I saw this giant Uncle Sam. He was carrying this bird cage, you know, just like the miners use to. Instead of canaries it was full of people. As he grew he would walk the land with the cage out in front of him. As the people began to die in the cage, he would turn and move in another direction. You see, he didn't give a damn about the people. His survival was all that mattered. If the government keeps it up, no one will be able to breathe. They will suffocate us all."

"You got more important things to worry about. You have to be at my house at 7:30 and I want you to show up sober. Got it?"

"Got it, I'll leave in a little while."

Chris got up and said, "7:30."

"OK, I'll be there." He watched her leave.

"Hey, Buddy, I'm gonna close up at 5:00." The bartender said.

"I'm leaving as soon as I finish this beer." Jesse answered.

As Jesse rose to put on his jacket he noticed that it had begun to snow. It was already dark. He said goodnight and walked to the door. As the door closed behind him, he was grabbed by both arms. Before he could even struggle he was knocked unconscious and thrown into a waiting black Ford Bronco. In less than thirty seconds they were gone. A man stepped from the side of the building lighting a cigarette. It was Michael Stewart.

Chris was worried. It was 9:00 PM. Her party was starting to wind down and still no Jesse. Booker walked over to her.

"Don't be worrying about him. He's probably made up with that woman you told me about and they're having a good time."

"I hope you're right. But he was adamant about being here tonight."

The men drove all the way to Deep Creek Lake. Jesse was unconscious for the entire trip. They turned onto a road just before the lake. The men remained silent until they pulled to a stop.

The driver said, "Drag his ass out." As soon as they pulled him from the car and the snow hit his face Jesse began to gain consciousness. They pushed him against the car. One of the men let go of Jesse to do something. At that instant Jesse kicked as hard as he could while pushing a second man who was by him. His kick struck the man in the side of the knee. Jesse heard bone crack and the man scream. Jesse ran as fast as he could. The man that he shoved regained his balance and pulled a revolver. He fired all six shots. Three struck Jesse, one in the right leg, one in the back and one in the head. Ralph Kolb, who had been driving the Bronco, came running.

"Jesus! You dumb ass, you've killed him. The boss said he wanted him hurt, not dead. Let's get the hell out of here." They left Jesse lying in the snow. Less than thirty minutes later a car came rolling up to where Jesse lay. The driver thought it was a deer lying in the road. He turned the flashers on and exited the car.

"Jesus!" The man, a state trooper, frantically checked Jesse for a pulse. He satisfied himself that Jesse was still alive and ran back to his car and retrieved a thermal blanket. He covered Jesse and then radioed for help.

"Adam 9, to dispatch."

"Go ahead Adam 9."

"I have a man down with multiple gunshot wounds. I need an ambulance immediately. I am at the entrance to Swallow Falls State Park. Tell them to drive in till they find us."

CHAPTER 57
WAITING AND WORRYING

To the sick, while there is life there is hope.

—*Cicero*

Chris had her scanner on in the kitchen. She heard the call for an ambulance. It was 10:00 PM and still nothing from Jesse. She was extremely worried. She had called the Starlite and the desk clerk had checked his room. He was not there. In fact the man said no one had driven in since it started snowing. It had began around 4:30 that afternoon. She was beside herself.

The ambulance arrived and they started to work on Jesse. One of the men stepped back with a shocked look on his face.

"You know who that guy is?"

"No," said the Trooper. "Who is he?"

"He's that new federal man. He was at our mine last week."

"Do you know his name?" The Trooper quizzed.

"Yeah, it's Jess Kamin."

The Trooper walked back to his car.

"Adam 9, to Dispatch."

"Go ahead A9."

"We've got a positive ID on the victim. His name is Jess Kamin."

Near midnight Chris Nolan's phone rang.

"Mrs. Nolan, this is Steve Vogel, from the state police. Your name was on the MSHA answering

265

machine for one of the emergency contacts. You were the only one that I could get a hold of. We are looking for the next of kin for a guy by the name of Jess Kamin."

"Is he dead?" A frantic Chris asked.

"He's alive but badly injured. They have him at Garrett Memorial."

"I'll stop at the office and get you the information. Can I take it to the hospital or do you want me to call you?"

"Please call us. The number is 387-1101."

Chris dressed quickly, only stopping long enough to call Booker.

When she arrived at the hospital she found Booker waiting for her.

"Have you heard anything yet?"

"Nope, they're still working on him."

They had a very long wait. It was 4:00 AM when the doctor finally came out to talk to them.

Walking straight to Chris he asked. "Are you part of his family?"

"No, Doctor, we work with him. The police are trying to get hold of his family now. Is he going to be alright?"

"Time will tell. We have removed the bullets."

Chris interrupted. "Bullets?"

"Yes, he was shot three times."

"God!"

The doctor put his hand on her shoulder. "He was very lucky. If it hadn't been freezing outside, he would have bled out. Two of the wounds, one in the back and the leg aren't life threatening, but he has a nasty head wound. Right now he's in a coma."

Booker stepped over to Chris and held her.

"It's time for prayers now." Booker said.

Christmas day, at 9:00 AM Buck Storm's phone rang. He walked into his den.

He barked, "Hello."

Ralph Kolb was on the line. "We took care of that problem for you. You won't be bothered again."

"Meet me at the mine in the morning. We'll settle up."

Buck hung the phone up and turned to find Billy standing in the door.

"Can't even get away from business on Christmas day, Pop?"

"Listen, boy. You had better learn that you always have to take care of business. 'Cause there's always someone out there who wants what you got."

Billy stood there shaking his head. "People aren't like that, Pop. They just want to be happy and make a living for their families."

"I want you to pay attention, boy. When I was a kid my grandpa took me to his mine. There we found one of his workers abusing one of his mules. My grandpa horse-whipped that fella, then he pulled me aside and gave me a bit of wisdom. He said them white niggers are a dime a dozen, but that mule is our life's blood. I don't let know one suck blood from my family."

"But that was a different time, Pop. It's not like that anymore."

"Don't kid yourself, boy. There is them that does and them that does for. That ain't ever gonna change."

At 4:00 PM on Christmas day Beth Stewart's phone rang. She answered.

"Hello."

"I'd like to speak to Beth Stewart."

"Speaking."

"This is Chris Nolan. I work with Jess Kamin."

Annoyed, Beth answered with a curt, "Yes."

"I wanted to let you know that Jess was shot last night. He is in Memorial hospital. They aren't sure if he will make it."

Beth never answered her. She let the phone fall from her hands. When she recovered her wits she called Midge. She asked Midge to go with her to pickup her kids. They were at her husband's house. She did not tell her why.

Beth heard the car pull up, and she quickly went outside.

"Midge, remember, that guy we had lunch with at the Wisp."

Midge shook her head yes.

"Someone shot him last night."

Midge was surprised, but did not show it.

"I thought you were through with him." Midge queried.

"One minute, I want him. The next, I don't. Look at what he did to Michael."

"You should have just screwed him and been done with it. I know you and how emotional you get. Especially when someone is hurt. Now don't do anything stupid, like marrying him, if he survives." They were just pulling up to Michael Stewart's home.

Beth answered as she was getting out of the car. "Don't worry, I'll be right back."

When she got to the door, she found the door partially opened. She knocked, but no one came. She pushed the door open and walked in. She could hear the kids yelling and laughing up stairs. She walked to the door of Michael's den and found him on the phone.

He had his back to her and was unaware of her presence.

She heard Michael say. "What do you mean you want paid? The son-of-a-bitch is still alive. (pause) I told you I wanted Kamin dead, he isn't. (pause) Go to hell."

Beth was stunned. She leaned back against the wall trying to regain her composure. When she heard him slam the phone down she quickly went to the front door and knocked loudly.

Michael walked into view. "Kind of early aren't you?"

Beth showed no emotion. "A friend of mine was injured and I need to go to the hospital. Midge is going to watch the kids."

"Who's the friend?"

"No one you would know." They both knew that she was lying.

CHAPTER 58
DESTINY'S CIRCLE

*Destiny is not a matter of chance; it is a matter of choice;
it is not a thing to be waited for, it is a thing to be
achieved.*

—W. J. Bryan, Speech, 1899

The following day at Buck Storm's mine a nervous
Ralph Kolb waited for Buck to arrive. He was talking
to his brother when Storm came roaring in. Ralph
could see that Buck was as mean as ever.

Hesitantly he said. "Mr. Storm, it's done. You won't
be bothered by that federal man again."

Storm was not smiling. "I thought I told you I didn't
want him dead."

"One of the guys got carried away. Kamin broke one
man's leg and was escaping when he was shot. He
didn't see anything. We took the guy that was hurt to
Kaiser to get his leg fixed. As soon as the doctor was
finished I paid them off and they were gone."

While they were talking, a rock truck upset in the
background. Buck turned at the noise to see men
running to the truck. Buck said to Bart Kolb, the
foreman, "When you get down there, tell that son-of-a-
bitch he's fired."

Kolb stunned asked. "Don't you want to see if he's
hurt first?"

"Don't get smart with me or you'll be out on your
ass with him."

Kolb glared at Buck, but did not talk back. He saw

271

the men pulling the uninjured man from the truck. He walked over and did what he had to do.

The shaken truck driver ran up to Storm. "Mr. Storm it wasn't my fault. I told you the steering was bad. It locked up."

Buck was in a nasty mood. "You're fired. Now get the hell off my job."

Buck turned to Ralph Kolb. "You're my new truck driver. Do you think you can handle it?"

"Sure, Mr. Storm, thanks."

"Let's just say it's a bonus for taking care of my problem."

CHAPTER 59
THE ACCOUNTING

Whoso diggeth a pit shall fall therein.

—*Proverbs, XXVI. 27*

The waiting room was crowded with friends and relatives of Jesse, his mother, her husband, and three of his sisters. Chris Nolan, Booker Katts, and Paul Barnes were also there. They all had worried looks on their faces. When the door to intensive care opened they all turned to face the doctor. He walked directly up to Jesse's mom.

"Your son is resting comfortably and in no immediate danger. I would like for all of you to go home and get some rest. It will be a long while before we know anything."

As they were about to leave Beth Stewart walked in. Chris Nolan greeted her.

"How is Jess?" Beth asked.

"They still don't know. They are sending all of us home to get some rest. The doctor said that he is in no immediate danger."

"I'll stay till you get back. How about giving me your telephone number and I'll call if there is any change."

Beth never talked to any of the others. She was ashamed that her ex-husband had caused this. She sat for several hours waiting for any word. She then noticed that the two nurses on duty stopped for a bite to eat. She quietly slipped into Jesse's room. What she saw frightened her. His head was bandaged, he had several IV's attached to him, and he was on oxygen. With tears in her eyes she went over to him. She held his hand. Her thoughts and emotions were running wild. She thought, I like this man. We could be great friends. It's just that he wants more. He wants love and I want friendship. I am going to redeem myself in front of all Garrett County. I don't need a husband to do it.

Then she was jerked from her thoughts. Jesse was squeezing her hand. She glanced up and saw his eyes half open.

"Doctor! Doctor!" She began screaming, running into the hall.

Chris Nolan's phone rang. "Hello." She answered. She put the phone down, whirling to the others. "Thank God, he's awake. He's going to be OK."

A week after the shooting everything was returning to normal, except Beth Stewart's conscience. She was plagued with guilt. It is what drove her to this moment. She had just pulled up to Michael Stewart's home. She knocked and heard Michael. When he opened the door his face lit up. "Well, hi."

Curtly, "Michael, we need to talk."

"This sounds serious."

"It is."

Michael began to eye her warily. "What the hell is it this time?"

"I know it was you that tried to have Jess Kamin killed." For the first time in her life she could see that she had power over him.

"I don't know what the hell you're talking about."

"On Christmas day, I overheard your call, with whoever you hired."

Acting as if nothing was wrong he responded. "Where do you suggest we go from here?"

"I have written a letter detailing everything. If anything should ever happen to me, it goes to the police."

"How could you think that I could ever hurt you?"

"I don't know you anymore. If you ever come near me or bother me again, it goes to the police. You understand?"

He looked at her with a cold smile.

"Do you understand?"

A few miles away at Garrett Memorial Jesse was dressing when a knock came at the door.

"Come in."

The doctor walked in accompanied by his nurse. He was reluctant to let Jesse leave the hospital but there was no holding Jesse.

"Mr. Kamin, we are letting you go home today, but you must promise me that you will rest. Please don't exert yourself."

Jesse thought to himself. Does he think I'll start jogging or something?

"Don't worry, Doc. There is only one activity that interests me. That's finding who did this to me."

"That's exactly what I'm advising against."

"I'll take care of myself, Doc, I promise."

"If you don't, you'll find yourself right back here."

He watched the doctor leave and sat back on the bed thinking. Chris had told him that Beth was here the night he awoke. She had never returned. He was going to make it a priority to see her. His thoughts were interrupted by the nurse who had returned with a wheelchair. She was accompanied by Booker.

The nurse smiled, "You get a free ride this time, Mr. Kamin."

"I told ya that you needed to slow down, boy. But I never thought we'd be pushing ya." Booker said. The nurse was laughing now.

CHAPTER 60
DO I OR DON'T I?

Man loves little and often, woman much and rarely.

—Giorgio Basta

Two weeks after Jesse was released from the hospital, he had tried to contact Beth Stewart without success. His family had returned to Ohio, after helping him find an apartment. He sat in the dark wondering why. Why would Beth not talk to him? Why did Midge keep hounding him? Why had someone wanted him dead? He spent another day brooding.

What Jesse did not know was that Beth was doing a little bit of soul searching herself. She confided in Midge.

Beth said, "He's been trying to call me. Everyday another call, I refuse to answer. If I did, he would take it as a signal that I wanted him more than a friend. I have things to do. I don't have time for a relationship. He's one of the few people that I can't be friends with. He can't separate friendship from love."

Midge burst out laughing. "I told you screw him and forget him."

"If I had gone to bed with him, I would never have gotten rid of him. He'd be like a stray dog. Feed him and you have him forever."

Midge, said with bitterness. "It really doesn't work that way. He'd probably never call you again."

Beth did not notice the sarcasm in her voice.

"I have to talk to him. I can't leave him hanging like

this. I have to make him hate me. I tried calling him at the motel, but they said he left. I think I'll call his office. They will know where to reach him."

Jesse sat in front of Chris's desk nursing a cup of coffee.

"Beth called me last night. She made it clear that she's not buying what I'm selling. Whatever the hell that means. How did she put it? Oh, yeah, Jess, you're a nice guy, but there are a lot of nice guys in this world. Stay safe and stay away from me."

Chris tried to sympathize with him. "Jess, if it's that hard, it ain't worth it. Love is supposed to come easy."

"Yeah, maybe you're right, anyway I got more important things to attend to."

Chris eyed him warily, "Don't tell me you're on that kick again."

"What kick is that?"

"You know what I mean. Like trying to find out who shot you. Let the police handle it, before you get yourself killed."

"Chris, you worry too much."

CHAPTER 61
YOU REAP WHAT YOU SOW

Every man meets his Waterloo at last.

—Wendell Phillips

Buck Storm drove into his pit to find all his men standing around a salamander trying to keep warm. It was the only way to keep warm on a morning like this. The salamander had a tub full of fuel oil and a chimney. You lit the fuel oil and before long you were being scorched on one side and freezing on the other.

"What the hell is going on?" Buck yelled.

Bart Kolb answered him. "Buck, it's near zero."

Buck looked around at the men. "You boys want to work or go home. There are at least ten men looking for each of your jobs. You decide."

The men slowly moved to their machines. Buck yelled for his son, who was still sitting in the pickup. "Hey, Billy, get on that end dump." He pointed to a Euclid rock truck. The boy never answered but moved immediately.

"What's wrong with that one?" Buck said pointing to another truck.

Ralph Kolb spoke up. "It's got a broken airline, Buck, no brakes."

"It's a piss poor truck driver that needs brakes. Plug the line." Buck was in a nasty mood.

Bart Kolb watched his brother move towards the truck. He turned to Storm. "One of these days you're going to get somebody killed."

"If you don't like it, you can get the hell out." Buck bit hard on his cigar and walked away. He had a habit of parking on the highest point in the pit and watching over the job, like a feudal lord watching over his serfs. He sat there most of the morning. He never thought about the comfort of the men but his heater was on full blast. He was not about to get cold.

They were using three rock trucks that day. A Caterpillar 992 front end loader was loading the machines. They were nearing the coal seam and had to transgress a long ramp to exit the pit. As usual Buck had seen no need to place berms along the edge of the road. The ramp was only wide enough for one truck. Later that day Billy was coming out of the pit and lost his engine. The air brakes automatically set. He climbed down the ladder and started to walk up the ramp to let Bart Kolb know. Then Ralph Kolb turned down the ramp. He saw the truck and Billy walking towards him. He instinctively tramped on the brakes. He had forgotten that the airline was plugged and he did not have brakes. Bart Kolb and the rest of the workers heard the crash. Storm drove his truck straight to the pit. He saw Billy's truck parked on the ramp and Ralph's lying on its roof. He got out of the truck and ran as fast as he could. He found Billy lying among the rocks. He cradled his son's broken body, as visions of the two children he had killed and the woman he had enslaved clouded his mind. A great agonizing sound came forth from Buck Storm, as he mourned the child he loved.

Jesse had been talking to Chris most of the morning.

"I almost forgot why I came in here. Do you have my check?"

"Yeah, it came in."

As they were talking Barnes came in.

"You got a minute, Jess?" They walked back to Barnes's office.

"Did the doctor give you a release date yet? We could sure use your help."

"Yeah, he said that he would release me in a month or so. I feel pretty good but I still have a problem with headaches."

In the background he could hear Booker and Chris joking around. He would rather be with them.

"When you're ready I'll send Booker with you. He can do the driving for a couple of weeks."

Jesse heard the phone ring and did not pay much attention until Chris yelled back.

"Paul, it's for you, the State Police."

Jesse saw the expression on Barnes's face change and the color drained from him.

"Yes, we will be right there." Barnes answered.

He turned to Jesse. "Storm's mine just had a fatal accident. Two men are dead."

"I want you and Booker to go with me. I know that you haven't been released to return to work yet, but I could use your help." He got back on the phone to notify the District of the fatalities.

When they arrived at the mine they found that the bodies had been removed. Barnes spoke to the State policeman while Jesse walked over to where the men were standing. They were congregated around the same salamander where they started their day.

"Hi, guys. Who was it?" He was shocked to hear that it was Storm's son and Bart Kolb's brother.

As he was walking back to Barnes he overheard one of them say, "Maybe if we had listened to that man

Ralph and Billy would still be alive."

They were standing in the bitter cold, with Storm being questioned by Barnes. Jesse did not hear what Barnes had asked. But Storm's answer roiled him.

"Do you realize how much I had invested in that boy?"

He then noticed Bart Kolb standing off by himself. The man was crying. Jesse should have consoled him, but he just could not. Suddenly, Kolb ran forward screaming. "You killed them, you killed them!" It took both State Troopers to keep Kolb from attacking Storm. Jesse was satisfied that this time at least MSHA would know exactly what happened.

He spied Booker talking to one of the men. He walked over to him.

"Can I have the keys, Booker?" Without a word Booker gave him the keys. Within a few minutes Barnes and Booker returned to the car.

Booker spoke first. "One of the men said that one of the trucks did not have brakes. The boy's truck stalled and he was walking up the ramp for help. The other truck started towards him. Without brakes he could not stop. I guess he tried to save the boy by running off the road. The boy panicked and moved the wrong way. The truck hit him and rolled forty feet into the pit."

Barnes just shook his head. He had never been on an investigation before where the victims were family members.

Barnes said, "Booker, I want you to take Jess back to Oakland. The State Police said they would stay till the District investigation team gets here. I'll stay with them."

Booker spoke. "Do you want me to come back?"

"No, not today, you can come back out with the team

tomorrow. They'll get me back to Oakland."

As they traveled back to Westernport and started up Route 135, Jesse was lost in thought. He was unaware of their ride up Backbone Mountain. He did not see the open land and forest on the mountain top. His only thought was how horrible it was for a man to cause the death of his own son, even if it was an accident.

"You know, Booker. All my life I've felt like a marble on the rim of a funnel. No matter what I said or did I was going down that hole. Maybe Storm was riding his own funnel. I despise that man and I feel sorry for him at the same time."

Booker thought for a moment. "Maybe he was a lost soul. We never know what a man goes through in life. I heard one time that our lives are the sum total of all our choices. He chose wrong. Remember that when you return to your briar patch jumping ways."

Jesse deep in thought finally said, "I think I'll try one more time with Beth. Who knows?"

Made in the USA
Charleston, SC
31 December 2012